THE
ESTUARY

DAVID REES

THE ESTUARY

GAY
MEN'S
PRESS

First published April 1983 by Gay Men's Press, PO Box 247, London N15 6RW

British Library/Library of Congress Cataloguing in Publication Data

Rees, David, *1936–*
    The estuary.
    I. Title
    823'.914 /F/   PR6068.E368

ISBN 0 907040 20 9

The quotation from *The Estuary* by Patricia Beer appears by
permission of Macmillan and Co. Ltd., and the quotation from
Murder in the Cathedral by T.S. Eliot by permission of Faber and
Faber Ltd.

Cover Art Graham Ward

Photoset by M C Typeset, 10 New Road, Rochester, Kent ME1 1BL
Printed by Book Plan (Billing & Sons Ltd), Worcester

for Matthias Daumann, with love

No one can really taste or smell
Where the salt starts but at one point
The first building looks out to sea
And the two sides of the river
Are forced apart by cold light
And wind and different grasses.

Patricia Beer, *The Estuary*

And I have found Demetrius like a jewel,
Mine own, and not mine own.

Shakespeare, *A Midsummer Night's Dream*

Nothing lasts, but the wheel turns,
The nest is rifled, and the bird mourns.

T.S. Eliot, *Murder in the Cathedral*

Chapter One

"Why don't we get married, then?"

The question, almost a little petulant when asked a second time, echoed in Cheryl's head all day, as she ran, late, for the bus; over coffee and at lunch; as she typed (Dear Mr. Howarth, I refer to my letters of the 26th February and the 25th March and still do not appear to have received the interest payment due for December. Please arrange to forward a remittance for £184.38 as soon as possible. Yours sincerely, A.T. Hodgson, District Manager); but as the day wore on – maybe it was the excessive heat even for July – the answers, for, against, or I don't know, came less frequently, or not so lengthily, and other, more immediate but easier problems pushed their way in and sorted themselves out, such as would Aaron mind chops for dinner two days running; should she do the washing this evening or leave it till tomorrow?

The heat had woken her early – five to six the clock, incredibly, was telling her – and as she lay, still half asleep and trying to remember her dream of tramping over wet ground, the moor she supposed, with Luke, both searching for – what? a horse? – Aaron had stirred, got up and gone out to the loo. When he returned they talked desultorily of unimportant things. He was tired; only four hours' sleep after a gig (how she hated that word, and his using it as easily as please and thank you). Aaron's Rod was on the downturn of the wheel, out of the charts for several months now; the girls didn't scream any longer. He nestled against her and was soon aroused; they made love but it was mild and ineffectual, he in his weariness no more than a gentle slithering inside her, and she still thinking of Luke. "Why don't we get married, then?" he'd asked, and all she'd answered was "mmmmm." She must have fallen asleep, for the next thing she knew was Ron standing beside the bed, switching off the alarm clock, and repeating his question. He waited, a towel in his hand. Sleek beautiful cat.

"All right."

"All right? Is that all you can say?" She smiled. "Good," he said, laughing, and he kissed her.

He dressed, old jeans and tee-shirt, but when he put on his leather jacket and started to check his pockets for money, keys and handkerchief, she realised he was going out.

"I have to see Kenny about a recording contract," he explained. "Had you forgotten?"

She listened to him banging about in the kitchen making breakfast. Fruit juice, coffee, toast and marmalade it would be: it never varied when he foraged for himself, though when they had time she cooked him smoked haddock or kippers or mackerel, always some kind of fish. It was his most recent fad. The door slammed and he was gone.

Did he mean it seriously? And was her "yes" serious? Their relationship had flourished because it had been cool, so completely lacking in the grand passion. It was the only kind of affair she could have endured after finishing with Luke. Certainly at the start, Ron had led her into it with great subtlety, knowing better than anybody else what had happened, watching all the stages of the break-up step by step, the rows, the studied calm, the walking-out and returning, the final bit of the disaster when Luke had coldly, almost savagely, packed up his things and gone for good. Ron, their landlord, hearing and seeing it all from upstairs, knew exactly how to comfort her, and after the weeks had gone by, how to persuade her to move in with him.

Often he was away for days at a time. The group still had engagements everywhere, Manchester and Liverpool last week, Birmingham and Cardiff the week before; and two months ago they'd flown to Copenhagen for five days. He often asked her to go with him, but the invitation never seemed to suggest his whole life depended on it, and she usually declined. Rock concerts every night did not appeal to her at all, and, besides, there was her job; not much of a job perhaps, a clerk in the Peckham Rye branch of the Halifax Building Society, but the first permanent job she'd ever had. After two years of casual work and unemployment benefit she was determined to hold on to it, though the money was not important; Aaron, at twenty-four, had already made a tidy sum from his career as a singer, and owned a cottage on the Exe estuary in Devon as well as the house they lived in at Greenwich. They lived very well. He said, once or twice, that it was unnecessary for her to work at all if she did not want to, but she answered, quite forcefully for her, that she did want to, thank you. It was hers, her own, her one and only independent piece of existence, and, after two years of Luke during which nothing, no decision, no opinion, no shred of herself seemed to be her own any longer but had been battered and twisted into being an inferior appendage of his, this area of life, quite separate from anyone else's influence, was enormously important.

She didn't mind Aaron being away. The solitude, the household chores, the occasional evening with Jack and Kevin, who'd moved into the downstairs flat, were more than adequate compensation for his absence. If he was there all the time she wouldn't like it; they would become tied up, she felt, in a complexity she didn't need, the sort of messy tangle that Luke had left her incapable of dealing with. Jack and Kevin were no complication, being gay: for her, an easy relaxed friendship with no sexual undertones to worry about. And Aaron, when he was there, exactly suited her. He wanted complete rest after the rigours of the club or disco, a home to sit in and drift about in slowly and, presiding over it, a girl who was housekeeper, bed-warmer, undemanding companion who let him unwind. Most other people would be horrified, she knew, by such a male chauvinist, but it was what she wanted. And his money gave her security after two years on Luke's grant and her meagre earnings: gone were the times when she did not know how next week's rent would be paid, or whether her last pound should go in the pub as Luke suggested, or washing clothes at the launderette, as she felt it should. Now there was every gadget in the kitchen she could possibly need, and thick carpets and good furniture, like being back at her parents' home, the farm on the edge of Dartmoor; more than that: meals out, expensive presents, weekends at the cottage, a holiday last Easter in Paris.

As a lover . . . She usually pushed this out of her head. Comparisons were uncomfortable. She had given herself totally to Luke. It wasn't that she still loved him; indifference, after a period of hatred, was all she felt now, but after Luke, nothing would ever be quite the same. If she was told she would die tomorrow, she'd say that the most completely happy moments of her life had been the best six or seven times in bed with Luke, and, yes, they, if nothing else, had made her life worth living. It wasn't always perfection, of course. She remembered a fragment of a poem he was fond of quoting, had used more than once to hurt her with:

> Harry, do they ever collide?
> I do not think it has ever happened,
> Oh my bride, my bride.

He would say it sometimes as if he was asking the opinion of the dead father he still mourned who was also called Harry.

Aaron, however, was physically the most beautiful man she'd ever met. Slim, lithe; peach-coloured skin: almost albino blond hair. Sexy: she couldn't exactly pin down what she meant by this word; it was ultimately something quite indefinable about him. She loved watching him, as she never had Luke: dancing, lifting a saucepan lid on the stove, driving the car, in bed lying on his back staring at nothing. Strange how different they were, the two lovers she'd had, not only as people, but even the minute bodily details – Luke, luxuriant hair from throat to toe, tufts of it peeping out from the top of his vests, while Aaron was all smooth skin: the weight of their bones and flesh, the thickness of a leg, even the amount they sweated, their smells, the curve of an arm. Luke, bigger, heavier, more . . . searching. So, she assumed, every single body, the more one read it and learned it, was as vastly different one from another as mind, heart, character.

Ron was out when she returned from work. Instead of peeling potatoes for dinner as she normally did, she poured herself a drink – gin, with tonic and ice – and sat in the window-seat of the living-room, staring out at the view. The house, a modest Victorian building, stood at the far corner of Blackheath, but at the rear the land fell sharply, and there was a spectacular view over the roof-tops of Greenwich. Close to was the spire of Hawksmoor's superb church and the rigging of the Cutty Sark; in the middle Tower Bridge and the dome of St. Paul's, both toy-size, and beyond, grey and shimmering in the heat and merging with a sky that also seemed grey at its edges, the hills of North London, Hampstead and Highgate. The downstairs flat had no such outlook. When she and Luke had lived there she was frequently irritated by the brick wall at the end of the garden that shut out this panorama; knowing what she was missing was worse than living in an area that had no view at all. Now it was hers.

Life with Aaron, she was sure, was a good recipe for two young people who had decided to live together, but who realised, even if it was unsaid, that in about a year they'd part, probably quite amicably, for other lovers, other modes of existence. There was something too much of the present about him, an instant, packaged, built-in obsolescence; he was a man with no sense of the past, no roots, no ties. Ron had asked her; why had she agreed? Easier than saying no? More than that: it was, to a large extent, what she also wanted. They weren't married yet. She could always change her mind.

His key turned in the lock. He was bearing gifts: a bottle of champagne, a bunch of red roses. Absurdly traditional for packaged obsolescent man! Or was it? As in a women's magazine, he was someone playing out the expected role. But it was sweet all the same.

"I thought we should celebrate," he said. He kissed her, no gentle parting or meeting kiss, nor the careful sensuality he sometimes used in bed, but a clumsy warmth that he hardly ever showed.

Yes. She would marry him. Provided the pattern of their lives did not change.

"Amen!" The final chords of *Zadok the Priest;* wild enthusiastic clapping such as is only heard at a Prom. John turned to Luke, laughed, and shouted over the noise, "It's not that good a piece of music!"

"It is! The most tremendous piece of instant drama ever written!" The conductor re-appeared, waved the choir into standing again, and the applause and cheering were once more tumultuous. Luke, flushed, sweating, moved more than he ever dared show, let out his emotions in thumping his hands and yelling "Encore!"

"Well, it suits you," John said when the hubbub had died away. The buzz of conversation started; the orchestra tuned their instruments. "All dramatic and ceremonial."

"Rubbish."

"Zadok the priest and Nathan the prophet anointed Luke king."

11

Luke smiled. "Odd concert, this."

"What? Sibelius and Handel as bedfellows?"

"Yes. Do you like this next piece?"

"Very much." It was the Sibelius second symphony. "Do you?"

"So-so. I prefer the fourth and the seventh. Best of all's the sixth."

"Snob."

"Why?"

"Just because this is the pop one. What about the eighth?"

"He destroyed it. Didn't you know?"

"He wrote the opening theme on a postcard and sent it to somebody. I thought you'd probably say it was his masterpiece, that theme."

"Idiot! Terrible, destroying a work of art. Like killing a child! Lady Churchill destroying that portrait. Senseless! Criminal!"

The conductor held up his baton. Silence. The music began: unhurried serene D major chords. John settled as close to Luke as he could without making it too obvious : their elbows touched, and their legs and hands. They were standing near the front of the Promenade, not as near the rail as they usually were, for tonight they'd been late : they were both fanatics, had season tickets, had missed only two concerts during the last six weeks.

At first, after the break-up with Cheryl, it had seemed easier going with men, and different, an experience that wouldn't lead to the same messy complications. It had started quite by chance, in a public lavatory; Luke, quite ignorant of cottages, was simply having a pee. The interest of a slim young man, a foreigner, Spanish or Italian he guessed, had been obvious, and extremely randy after days without sex he had allowed himself to be led on to the common : the youth kneeled on the grass and sucked him off, very efficiently. I'll choke the kid, he thought, as he shot into the expert mouth. "Thanks," the boy whispered, and vanished into the night. It was the only word that had been spoken.

Luke expected to feel disgust, but he did not. Surprised, and not really aware of possible danger, he went back to the same toilet several times in the next few weeks; but the boy was never there. He went with other men, but it wasn't as satisfactory as that first time. However, leaning against the same tree and feeling big, macho and superior, he enjoyed the quick, anonymous, needed physical relief. It gave him time to get on with other things : finals

12

were near. He thought a great deal about what was happening to himself: was he gay? No: there was no sudden change in what he felt for women. But he liked the male hands touching his skin, the firm flesh of a man's body. Though he wasn't sure what to do with what he was offered. Mostly, he let them get on with it : sucking, tossing him off; he wasn't ready for anything more intimate. If that boy returned . . . well, it might be different. One evening he went over to Greenwich to see Jack and Kevin; they were amazed at what he told them, alarmed almost. All the assumptions they'd made about him now had to be re-examined; a piece of their social structure wasn't what they had always known. Luke was amused by their reactions. "I'd certainly like to know who this foreign kid is," Jack said. "He must be God's gift to the gay world if he can turn you – of all people! – off the straight and narrow! It's incredible!"

"I don't understand it," Kevin said.

"I don't understand it either," Luke answered.

"Are you worried?"

"No. Why should I be?"

"I would be, if I suddenly started to fancy women."

Jack raised an eyebrow, and said, sarcastically, "Save me the bother, wouldn't it!"

Kevin ignored that, and said to Luke, "What would you do if somebody wanted to fuck you?"

Luke shuddered. "Run a mile."

"You want to screw *him*?"

"Who?"

"This boy."

Luke smiled. "Maybe," he said, after a moment.

In the Prom queue, the first Beethoven evening, Luke saw him. His heart turned over. The blood thumped. Only a few paces ahead, with a crowd of friends; not a foreigner, judging from the way he spoke – a flat London accent – just very dark-skinned. Slight, good-looking, black hair, girlish : no, not girlish– waif-like. Vulnerable. Their eyes met. A question in the look, recognition; then he turned away. When the doors opened Luke lost him in the rush for the front. The fourth piano concerto went unheard, a favourite piece every note of which he knew and loved. He found himself clapping, not knowing how or why they had arrived so suddenly at the last G major chord.

Someone pushed a piece of paper into his hand. He looked up :

13

the boy was moving away from him, edging between people packed close as sardines, struggling to return to his friends. Luke glanced at what he was holding. "See you afterwards? They're all coming back for coffee, but do take care; they're straight. John."

Luke, in John's living-room, said very little. He was too embarrassed, trying hard to suppress an urge to make an excuse and run away. But the friends weren't curious; they just accepted him as another young music-lover. They had all met quite recently, boy or girl standing close together in the Prom queue. Luke concentrated on the details of the room, books and furniture, records, vast quantities of pottery; and he answered questions he was asked as briefly as he could. John was the maker of all the pots, he discovered. And a lot older than he had thought; must be, to afford such a flat. When the others left Luke pretended to be staring very hard at the words on a record sleeve.

Ten minutes later they were in bed. The screwing is fantastic, Luke thought sleepily at two a.m.; why on earth didn't I find that out years ago?

In the morning he got up and left for work so silently John did not hear him, but there was a note on the bedside table : "Back at half past five," and another on the stove in the kitchen : "I shall count the minutes." Since then Luke had not spent another night in his own bed-sit, but he must have been there once, a week later, for he returned from work one evening with all his possessions. "It seems crazy forking out two lots of rent," he said. "Is it all right? I'll pay half." John nodded, smiling. Luke's possessions : next to nothing. He'd said once that everything he owned he'd had to struggle for, but John had not realised how poor he actually was. A record-player, clothes — mostly patched jeans, tee-shirts, and sneakers — a few books, squash and tennis racquets. "Not much," Luke said, reading his thoughts. "I did tell you. There's the car outside, of course." John had not yet ventured out in this dangerous-looking vehicle, a very ancient Mini that had belonged to Luke's brother; Adam, Luke explained, could hardly take it with him to Australia. In the last three years almost every bit of it had needed repair or renewal. He'd taught himself how to do it; there was little, he boasted, about that car he had not laboured on. And it still worked.

Luke was much too young for anything permanent, of course. Despite the life they had begun to share. Nine years his junior, not

14

even really gay. John was thirty, a little soured by experience, but amused and flattered he'd been mistaken for seventeen or eighteen. And Luke was attractive all right, tall, with blue eyes and dark shoulder-length hair parted in the middle. A very male man : fit, muscular: a massive cock. Being screwed by Luke was something like perfection.

Only twenty-one he might be, but as a lover he was always intuitively right, as if he'd never been nervous or unsure in bed : or on the floor of the living-room, once in a dark corner of the Albert Hall (down in its depths after long unswept corridors), once when the concert had finished on the grass of the park beside a flower-bed of antirrhinums, all different dazzling colours. He was like a dancer, a skater, always searching for more than he knew and mostly succeeding, just as his body, particularly the broad back and long legs, was somehow just a little more to John's liking than almost any other man he had known. Yet they never discussed it (he didn't dare, fearing the probe would make Luke think of how long, or short, his stay would be, put a period to it at least), and talked not at all of "us" or "the future". Sometimes, thinking he sensed that John was anxious, Luke would write in the notes he left before going to work – a custom he kept up, not every day, but quite often – intended reassurances : "I need you. Look in bathroom," where there was a second note : "I know you need me. Don't worry about it." Sometimes the messages were coarser, but just as comforting. "You're the best fuck I've ever had" was written one morning in red letters on a piece of card on the mantelpiece, and, in smaller letters underneath, "Look in kitchen cupboard," where on top of a jar of Tesco's marmalade, was an unopened packet containing a dozen contraceptives and on a piece of paper, "I've had these for months, but somehow they don't seem to be necessary any longer! Throw them away." Best of all was a card he'd actually posted, a print of a Pre-Raphaelite painting from the Tate, a weeping girl in lurid colours, a man, jaws firmly set, leaving her; "*I'm* not leaving," he wrote. "Not for as long as I can see. Look on top of lavatory cistern," on which were the words, traced by his finger in the dust, "Clean me. If you don't I will. I love this flat."

Sibelius. Luke, absorbed, forgot John's presence; their elbows no longer touched. What do I know of this guy, John asked himself. They had one important thing in common : they were both orphans. But whereas he had no surviving relatives – only a family of second cousins in America, Luke had his married brother in Australia, an aunt he never saw who owned a fish-and-chip shop in New Cross, and cousins in Exeter, though he'd not heard of them for donkeys' years. His only ties and responsibilities were to himself. Just graduated in English from London University, and now employed by the London Borough of Haringey to cut grass verges with a motor mower. That was a joke, he said; there was remarkably little grass in the London Borough of Haringey that needed cutting. Most of the time he lazed about, getting sunburnt and looking looking butch. He'd been at London University because his 'A' levels weren't good enough for his first choice, Sussex. He had grand designs, great dreams: a journalist travelling round the world, sending dispatches from its hot spots. At the moment he was collecting rejection slips from every provincial and suburban newspaper he applied to, *Clarions, Gazettes* and *Expresses* in Willesden, Brighton, Peterborough, every bloody place. After the summer job it would be the dole. He was vastly enthusiastic about things; opinions and value judgements showered from him in waterfalls, on books, architecture, sport, music, politics: particularly music. It was a fine intellect, but wild and undisciplined. He'd had a trial for a junior England team, in squash of all things, when he was in this third term at university, but he hadn't been selected. There was a girl he'd lived with; it had started when he was still at school, but it broke up a year ago. Only two friends he really cared about, a gay couple who lived in Greenwich, both teachers.

John surfaced from his thoughts as the first movement finished. Fuck it! And he wondered if Luke perhaps wasn't right : maybe it *was* inferior to the later symphonies. No, no! He would *not* allow Luke to take him over so completely, jostling his views and ideas aside, implanting his own so insistently. "Wallpaper music," Luke whispered.

"Balls."

He concentrated himself firmly on the rest of the music. Yes, he was right and Luke was wrong. The black melancholy of the slow movement, the perfectly correct peroration of the last, a better, more satisfying *Finlandia*. He argued it lengthily when they were back home at the flat.

"I love the Albert Hall," Luke said, ignoring John's thesis.

"Those same stale coffee smells in the corridors every night. Do they ever clean it?" He was taking a record out of its sleeve. "And that funny thing dangling above the orchestra. Do they think for one moment it really improves the acoustics? And all us lovely young people jammed up together like a huge litter of smelly puppies. Now, listen to this."

"What is it?"

"The sixth. The landscape of the mind."

"Sibelius said that, not you."

"I know. But it *is* the landscape of the mind. Mental space."

John listened from the kitchen, washing up saucepans from their evening meal, making coffee. Luke took off his socks and shoes, then sprawled on the sofa, lost in the music.

A rolling stone of twenty-one, a penniless dreamer; in a month, maybe two, maybe three, he'd move on. It was a certainty. At work John would convince himself of his stupidity, that it couldn't last, that he'd crash down to earth with a sickening bump, that life, after Luke, would be an aching emptiness, without point or meaning. Why the hell had he allowed himself to get involved? Luke would leave : he was so much younger.

On the first day of the summer holidays Kevin left for France, to attend a month's course at the University of Montpellier. Jack felt relief more than any other emotion: his lover's depressed moods had become very tiresome. He had patiently tried to understand, but gave up the attempt in some considerable irritation, an irritation partly with himself for his inability to be sympathetic. There seemed to be no coherent reasons for Kevin's unhappiness; the explanation to which he constantly recurred, that it was something to do with going to France, was unconvincing. He had gone of his own free will, on a course that was not imperative (though he had a degree in French he was a primary school teacher), had signed up for it, Jack suspected, because he needed a complete break: a holiday on his own, maybe a brief affair with somebody else, then a return, refreshed, to the old life. They had lived together for over four years, and their existence had perhaps become stale; they both needed new experiences. He was quite looking forward to the month's absence himself, had indeed become almost eager for it after the consequences of Kevin's depression: arguments, bouts of drunkenness with Kevin being sick all over the carpet or the bed, occasional outbursts of violence when Kevin had smashed plates or kicked him in the shins with his heavy wooden clogs.

Relief or not, the flat was unpleasantly empty without his lover, indeed made worse by the signs of Kevin having so recently gone, socks and knickers left in the corner of the bedroom, a stubbed-out cigarette, a letter from his sister with a brown stain on it where he had carelessly spilled a cup of tea. On the spur of the moment Jack asked Aaron if he could stay at the cottage for a few days. Aaron had no objection, and Cheryl, sensing why, fussed round, making tea, telling him to leave all the dirty washing with her. She came downstairs to help him pack.

"You're already missing him," she said. He did not answer. Cheryl he'd known since the time she'd started with Luke. She had watched or heard all the miseries and marvels of his affair with Kevin; indeed Kevin used her as a confidante, almost daily. He did not, preferring to talk to Luke, but Luke seemed to have disappeared for the time being; since the astonishing revelations of a few months ago, he had moved in with this potter – John, was it? – and Jack had heard from him only once, a brief phone conversation. He had only a vague idea of where Luke was living. Somewhere near the Albert Hall, he thought, but he'd lost the address. Cheryl did not necessarily prefer Kevin to Jack, despite their cosy chats over the ironing, or the two of them sewing cushion covers upstairs and drinking Aaron's whisky. She never took sides. She was a girl who found gay men a blessing, who wearied quickly of her own sex and felt straight males a constant threat; who found, therefore, gays the best kind of companions and friends. Well as Jack knew her, however, her decision to marry Aaron had been a complete surprise; she'd laughed at his bewilderment, presumably having anticipated it, just as she knew how to counter, in an unruffled way, Kevin's comments to the effect that she would regret it. Aaron he quite liked, not because of misplaced gratitude that his landlord didn't mind two gays under his own roof (the rent, after all, was paid regularly, and that was the basis of their knowing each other), but the liking stopped short of admiration. Nor did he allow his acknowledgement of Aaron's sexy good looks to cloud his judgement. Ron was one hundred per cent selfish. It would end up in a worse mess than her affair with Luke.

"Penny for your thoughts," she said.

"I was thinking about you, not Kevin."

"Were you?" She did not seem to believe him. "Do you have his address? I'll write in a day or two."

"It's on that pad by the phone."

She copied it down. "You could always ring him, I suppose."

"Could I?"

"If you wanted to. Cost the earth, of course, but . . . he's written the number on the other side of this piece of paper."

"Has he? He didn't say." Jack took it from her and looked at the row of figures. Maybe he would. It hadn't occurred to him to telephone such a far-off place as Montpellier.

"You go off and enjoy yourself. Don't be too promiscuous."

"Why should you think I intend to be promiscuous?"

"Kevin said he was hoping to meet a tall dark handsome Frenchman."

Jack grinned. "Well, *I* shan't. They're not so common on the Exe estuary as they are in Languedoc." He thought for a moment, frowning. "It's dangerous."

"What is?"

"Having casual sex while your partner's away. And I don't mean the risk of V.D."

"What then?"

"Getting involved."

"Mmm. Most gay couples do, don't they?"

"Some. Yes. Not all."

"But you haven't."

"No." But he might look in at the gay pub in Exeter, or the club at Torquay; there would be old friends it would be good to meet. And there was the nagging, uncomfortable thought of his parents. He said, "In fact, I'm wondering whether to pay my mother a visit."

"Are you?" She was surprised. Jack, hating the lies and deceptions, had told his parents a long time ago about himself and Kevin. They had taken it badly; his father, for a while, even going as far as refusing to allow Jack to come home at all. Not so his mother, though she would not tolerate Kevin arriving at the house. In consequence, Jack had kept away permanently. All three suffered, but no one would give in. To make matters worse, not long after the unpleasant scene when he had told them, his younger brother Owen had left home, saying the inhuman treatment they had meted out to Jack had made his own position untenable; he couldn't bear living with them, he said. Jack thought it was probably a convenient excuse rather than a good reason, but he felt guilty all the same at being a cause of further unhappiness. He appreciated Owen's support, however, and regretted that he hardly ever saw his brother these days. Owen operated a computer for some large firm in Edinburgh, earned a fortune, and had worked his way rapidly through dozens of girl-friends. At twenty-two he was a success.

"It's time this silly feud was brought to an end," Jack said. "So I might . . . well . . . open up preliminary negotiations."

"Without Kevin."

"If they won't accept him the negotiations will stay very preliminary."

"I wish you joy of it! I don't think you'll succeed."

"Neither do I."

"If you're going to Okehampton, will you call in and see *my* parents?"

"Of course. I was going to do that anyway."

"They know we're getting married. I was a whole *hour* on the phone about it! But they haven't actually seen us since I told them. Talking to you would be the next best thing, perhaps." She smiled. "Mum will give you dozens of messages and instructions. And we haven't even settled where it's going to be."

"What do they feel about Luke nowadays?"

After his father's death Luke had lived with Cheryl's parents. "I'm never really sure. They've lost touch, but that was his doing, not theirs."

"Will you ask him to the wedding?"

"Yes. I have to; he's almost their adopted son. You think I shouldn't?"

"What does Ron say?"

"His friend too. Sort of."

Neither Jack nor Kevin had mentioned to Cheryl that Luke was now interested in men. Would it upset her? Probably. He didn't like hiding things from her, so talking about Luke had recently become an embarrassment. He decided to change the subject. "You look good," he said. "Our healthy country girl! Black eyes, black hair, glowing cheeks . . . you could make gays wish they were straight." The words sounded stupid, false.

"Idiot. You're still the English sportsman type, aren't you! You could make straight men wish they were gay! Blond hair, white open-necked shirt. As if you've just come off the cricket field!"

"Why does everybody have to keep on saying *that*? I *hate* cricket!"

"Squash court, then."

"To think I could once beat Luke! I hardly dare ask him for a game now. He plays me sometimes, but it's a whitewash." Luke again! He was so much a part of their lives, past and present; they could never avoid him in their conversations. A fixture, a constant, that was no longer fixed or constant : it made Jack uneasy, as if it suggested the other props of his life weren't what they had always seemed.

She hesitated, then asked, "How will Kevin's looks strike the French?"

High cheekbones, dark curly hair. Green eyes. Beautiful. He said, non-committally, "His charm lets him get away with anything. Our Kevin Sullivan." He glanced at his watch. "I think I'd better go."

She kissed him. "Be good. Or rather, be careful. Do you want another cup of tea first?"

"No thanks. If I stay here much longer I'll turn into a tea-bag. You look after yourself."

"I will. Anyway, we might see you at the weekend. We might come down and destroy your privacy. Do you mind?"

"Of course not."

Nearly four hours later, late in the sleepy summer afternoon, he was sitting in the garden of the cottage staring out at the estuary. Cries of children, the rumble of a train, drifted to him from the distance. The tide was slipping out, letting the white boats sag sideways, exposing a bed of blotchy mud that made its own strange sound, quite inimitable, in part like the slosh of water, in part like dry sand or wind in reeds. Hundreds of birds stood motionless on the glistening flat slime, singly, in pairs, in dozens; gulls he recognized, but others astonished him by their alien shapes and colours, impressed him with his own ignorance. Exmouth looked friendly at the far end on the other side, its tall church tower dominating the houses; and the pattern of coloured fields draped on the hills opposite was warm, familiar, almost chocolate-box: like so much of the Devon he'd known since he could remember anything. Nevertheless he felt utterly remote here, on the edge of the estuary, lost almost. It was not an unpleasant sensation. The

Turf Inn, which still functioned as a lock cottage at the start of the canal, the oldest canal, centuries older than the Duke of Bridgewater's, was the nearest house, only a quarter of a mile away, but he couldn't see it from where he sat: it might as well have been as far off as London. Exeter, five or six miles up-river, seemed impossible. Though he'd probably drive there later. This slit of water, prizing the land open, was absorbing him into itself: I could live here, he thought. Kevin came into his mind, and he was hurt by the ache of absence: Kevin's skin tight on ribs like a drum-skin, the hollows between like finger-marks, the smooth boy's body. So slightly built, and looking younger than he was: the beauty of his maleness.

He went indoors and made tea, took it back to his deck-chair, and stared at the flowers of the garden: gaillardias, stocks. Sweet scents. Doubtless planted by Cheryl. He smoked a cigarette, and considered his loneliness. Then drifted to sleep. When he woke there seemed to be no water at all between him and the far side, but he supposed there must still be a thin trickle somewhere. I shan't sleep tonight, he said to himself; I never can when he's not beside me. He saw that the little white boats had sagged as far as they were able to, as if all life had been sucked out of them.

Chapter Two

Luke began to take more interest in the flat. It was the lack of a garden, he said, that bothered him, the absence of flowers; not that he had ever previously been perturbed one way or the other by matters horticultural. True, John had several indoor plants, trailing green things, and one rather impressive sort of ivy growing from a pot in a corner of the living-room which had almost succeeded in reaching the ceiling; but, here, on the top floor of this old Victorian house, something else was needed. The view from the windows at the back and the front was all roof-top, squares and oblongs of different shapes like an abstract painting; pleasant patterns, yes, but such dull colours: only the lines of washing showed that other similar attics in Queen's Gate, Prince Consort Road or Exhibition Road actually had people living in them.

He came home one evening with several tubs of flowers on the seats and in the boot of the Mini. "From one of Haringey's swimming-baths," he explained. "They're being replaced with fixed concrete tubs. That's my job, next few days: mixing concrete. Now help me upstairs with these."

"And they let you have them?"

"Not exactly." He staggered up the four flights of stairs, clutching a tub full of petunias to his chest. John followed, dragging the smallest, which contained French marigolds and a great deal of litter: discarded ice-cream wrappers and cigarette cartons.

"Where the hell do you think you're going to put them?"

"You'll see. We're going to have a garden where we can sunbathe." He stood on a chair and opened the trap-door in the kitchen ceiling; the roof above was flat. He heaved the tubs through, one by one. "There's several more," he said. "I'll fetch them now, I think, but it will take time. We'd miss the concert."

"Tchaikovsky. Which is too pop for you."

"I love *Swan Lake,* and the *Pathétique.* But they're not performing either."

"Oh go on, go and fetch your flowers. I'll cook some dinner."

So they obtained a garden of sorts. Luke threw out the most anaemic-looking plants, and replaced them with two small conifers, fuschias and geraniums. Some of these he bought; some, he said, were 'left-overs'. He inspected his new acquisitions each evening and watered them, for there had been no rain for days; but otherwise he had little time to spend on the roof except at week-ends or when they chose to eat up there. John used the roof more often than Luke did, on sunny afternoons when he wasn't working or out taking his pots to the various shops around London which stocked John Perry products; but it was Luke who discovered, by arranging the tubs round the edge of the roof, that it was possible to sunbathe in the nude, for they were now not overlooked by anyone. Once when he was up there, he heard John come home from the pottery; he had forgotten how late it was. He let himself through the hatch, and rested his elbows on the sides, poised to jump down to the kitchen floor. Fingers stroked his legs: he was instantly aroused. "Stay there," he said. Fingers caressing his balls; his cock in a mouth, sucked, slowly. It was exquisite, the sensation, all the more so because he couldn't see what was happening. He was looking at other people's windows, roof-tops and sky, and his sperm was flooding into someone's throat.

He jumped down and saw his lover, more waif-like than ever it seemed, in faded cords and a pink, tie-dyed tee-shirt. Luke almost ripped off the clothes. He kneeled, and used his mouth.

Afterwards John said, "You've never done that before."

"Was it good?"

"Christ! What do you think!"

"I love you." They stared at each other for several moments, astonished. Luke turned away. "We'll get some bulbs when the flowers die. They'll look good in the spring."

"I'm too old for you."

"No."

"You'll leave me —"

"Shut up!"

24

"You'll find a woman. Fall in love, marry her. Have children."
Luke hit him; John, touching his stinging face, said, "Why did you
do that?"

Luke, ashamed, stared down at the floor. "I . . . sometimes want
to hurt you. I don't know why."

"In bed?"

There was another long silence. "I . . . think you want me to."

"Maybe."

"You've never said . . . "

"What?"

"I love you."

John pulled on his trousers, found his tee-shirt on the draining-
board, and said "I won't commit. You'll leave me."

"You bastard."

"No. It's self-defence. Even if I might enjoy the other."

"Other?"

"Tell me about Cheryl."

"Why?"

"Because it's time to do so."

Luke sighed, went to the bathroom, then to the kitchen and
fiddled about with utensils in a drawer. "Where's the bloody
corkscrew?"

"In the usual place."

"Oh." He came back with two glasses of wine. "It's none of your
business," he said. "Is it?"

"Yes. It is."

"It doesn't show me in a very good light."

"I'd guessed that."

He'd pursued her for months when he was a sixth-former, had
practically bludgeoned her into an affair. Her parents had been
very good to him when his father died. When he'd come to
London with her at the beginning of his three years at the university
they'd continued to live together, in a series of unspeakable bed-
sits, then finally at Aaron's, their first decent flat, but with a rent they
could scarcely afford. To make ends meet he'd had casual jobs in
the holidays and behind a bar several nights a week in term-time;
that and his academic work left no time for the fun everybody else
seemed to be having. Cheryl became more and more insecure and
clinging, dreamed of engagement ring and wedding and two kids.
Yes of course he'd loved her. But the pressures strained and

snapped him. More and more he didn't want to settle down, craved for freedom. Unsatisfied lust for other obviously available girls. Two years of it: living on top of each other, no money, no break from routine, sex becoming more and more unsatisfactory. No intellectual rapport with her; she could not follow the way his mind grew. Not that that was desperately important, but it didn't help. So, rows and more rows, he going out drinking, then the first girl on the side. Not particularly interesting when he looked back on it, but at the time . . .! Then others. Cheryl found out, but it was he who ended it. Packed up everything one day and left. Not a pretty story, was it?

John didn't answer, waiting for him to go on. Freedom! At first it was like intoxication; parties, picking up girls, booze, indiscriminate sex. But freedom palled; sleeping around became hateful. The increasing sense of desperation that if he didn't take a girl to bed after a Saturday-night disco he was some kind of failure. It led to fastening on to anyone; he would wake up in the morning, and look and think how could he have done it? He'd caught gonorrhoea. Went straight to the clap clinic, had had no inhibitions about it. A few penicillin pills and he was cured. Lucky. Many cases were a lot more unpleasant than his. Then . . . that lavatory. It had given him time to work, and he *had* worked hard, got a better degree than he would have done if he'd stayed with Cheryl.

The last three years had left him a lot less sure of himself than he'd been at eighteen. He thought twice now about everything. No, he did really (for John laughed), particularly about relationships. He wasn't insecure, craving for love and affection. He was, simply, bewildered by his own behaviour. "Bewitched, buggered, and bewildered," he said. "Not quite, I suppose. You're the one who gets buggered."

"Luke, what honestly do we have? Screwing's perfect. Books, music, this flat, which you love, I don't know why. Enough for the next fifty years?"

"I love you. I said."

"It's too soon. For you. You're very sex-orientated."

"Meaning?"

"It seems to dominate you more than any other drive."

"I'm young, as you're so fond of telling me. All that testosterone whirling around inside me; I think I spent my adolescence in a state of permanent erection!"

"Do you want children?"

"Yes." He laughed. "Rather a contradiction, isn't it?"

"Perhaps."

Luke put on his clothes. "I don't really understand what's happened to me. I still don't think of myself as gay. I'm not!" He shook his head.

"What are you, then?"

"Bisexual. Obviously. But you . . . why should it be *you*? Yes, I might leave you. I might get married. Have children. I don't know, for Christ's sake! Saying I love you . . . it isn't a commitment. A promise. It's a statement of fact. John, it's just about the only fact I'm sure of!"

"Why this works . . . you and me . . . we don't put limits on each other's freedom. As soon as you start hemming in your lover's freedom, it starts going sour. But there are bound to be hundreds of things you don't want your lover to do."

"Such as if I went to bed with somebody else?"

"Not necessarily. Depends on why, not who."

"I don't follow that. Let's go over to Greenwich; I haven't seen Jack for weeks. I want you to meet him." He picked up the car keys.

Jack was profoundly ill at ease with himself. The whole experience had left him with a feeling that he had tampered with the natural order of things; but, if it had not happened, he knew he would be just as dissatisfied even though the reasons might be rather different. He had gone to the gay pub in Exeter the previous night. The crowd of students with whom he had associated when he was at the university had of course long since gone; in their place was a group of fresh-faced youngsters he'd never seen before, who looked him up and down, then returned to their own conversations. He found himself talking eventually to a man in his early twenties called Hugh, an attractive blond who was part-owner, with his mother, of a restaurant near Totnes. After closing-time Jack took him to the cottage.

In the car he told Hugh about Kevin. Obviously Hugh thought Jack more interesting than one night's fun, for, from that point on, the brightness ebbed from the conversation. Jack felt guilty; Hugh's hopes had evidently been dashed, and Hugh, he was certain, thought the less of him. The man deserved better treatment: amusing, intelligent, interesting; the kind of person he would choose if he was free and hoping to begin an exciting new relationship. Good-looking too, and, undressed, beautiful. This sense of being immoral towards Hugh and of being unfaithful to Kevin (no matter that Kevin might be doing exactly the same himself) spoiled their love-making; Jack was like a young teenager, so shy and unsure that, though he was able to finish at last, Hugh must have thought it hardly worthwhile. He apologised.

Hugh laughed, not unkindly, and said, "There's no need. I know precisely what you're going through. It's happened to me. Not now, but in the past." He kissed Jack, very gently. "Look – if things go wrong with Kevin . . . well, you said there were problems . . . I've told you where I live."

"Yes. I shan't forget."

"Let's sleep now."

Which he did, instantly, curled up like a question mark. Jack, however, did not sleep for a long time. And, in the morning, Hugh was in no hurry to leave, so they ended up driving down to the restaurant which was on another estuary, the Dart, and had lunch there; he met Hugh's mother, a delightful dotty woman who knew exactly what the score was with her son and didn't mind, and who made Jack very welcome, saying she hoped she'd see more of him, in between explaining the ways other restaurants swindled their customers and ruined meals with badly frozen vegetables and *coq au vin* out of tins.

"I *will* see you again," Jack said to Hugh. "I'll meet you tonight."

But at the cottage, alone and looking out over the estuary, as the tide once more leaked away like water slowly spilling from a bottle and the boats, without their prop, keeled over, he felt so much remorse, such a sense of being a cheat, that he hurried out and phoned Hugh, saying it was impossible, that he wouldn't see him, ever, unless Kevin left him for good. Hugh being so understanding merely twisted the knife, and the least Jack felt he could do was to agree to write in a few days' time.

He decided to go back to London, to be out of harm's way. What did this sudden attraction really mean? That something was radically wrong between him and Kevin that he hadn't realised? A four-year itch, or had all the magic gone, become lost in the routines of the existence they shared? He didn't know the answers, and Hugh's face kept popping up maddeningly in his mind's eye.

He packed. Then sat staring round him at the cottage. It was a tiny place, oddly shaped like a triangle that had had one of its apexes cut off, so that one wall in all its rooms was larger than its opposite. A flight of stairs just inside the front door led up to the two bedrooms (one double, one single); underneath the smaller were crammed three minute areas – kitchen, bathroom and loo – while to the left of the front door was the lounge, with its big picture-frame window looking out to the estuary. The most impressive part of the lounge, however, was a huge stone fireplace of Dartmoor granite: a surprise to find this material so far from the moor itself, and the lintel over the fire was a giant slab of it, the marks still visible where wedges had been hammered to make it split from a bigger, more shapeless mass of rock. This lintel fascinated him; he had never looked carefully at such a thing before. Primitive. And beautiful. He thought of the men who had put it there – there must have been several, considering its size – groaning under the weight as they heaved it into position. How did it stay up? He examined it; nothing pinned it to the chimney: it was simply resting on the smaller blocks of granite beneath, a filling of lime or some sort of ancient mortar between it and the next stone.

The cottage was damp, and infested with wood-lice, but he liked it. He envied Aaron's ability to write a cheque for the fifteen thousand pounds the place had cost. Like Ron he felt he needed a hideaway, a secret address. What shall I do now, he asked himself. Kevin! Oh why did you have to go away, lover? He'd phone the boy. Now. Why not? Was it possible to ring Montpellier from a call-box? He'd need about two or three pounds in 10p pieces, and, of course, he didn't have such a large number of coins. When he returned to London, perhaps. But he didn't want to return to London. What, then? Liverpool. Yes. Mike and Stuart. He'd always gone to Mike when he'd been in trouble, or lost and lonely like now, ever since they'd got to know each other in the first year at university. He thought of the house in Liverpool; warm, cheerful, and quite characterless on a new housing estate. Château Garswood they called it. He'd not been there since last Christmas (Christmas at home had not been possible for three years now) and he and Kevin had had a marvellous time, the four of them celebrating together, in the house or at the clubs with a gang of Mike's friends: strange Liverpudlian accents and easy companionship. Yes, he'd go up to Liverpool.

The sound of a car broke his thoughts. He looked out of the window: a Capri. Cheryl and Aaron.

It was a contract with EMI that had brought fame, fortune, and a considerable disruption in lifestyle to the members of Aaron's Rod. Aaron had started the group when he was seventeen: Danny Jones, the drummer, Guy Petersen, the lead guitar and back-up vocalist, and Dominic Hubbard, piano, had all been in the group from the beginning, were in the same form as Aaron at school. They'd played first at local parties and discos; then, when they were eighteen, they had left home and moved to London. For two years it was a hard unpleasant life: seedy rooms in the poorest parts of the city, few engagements, nobody of any importance in the music world taking any notice. They'd survived, but only because they had inordinate faith in themselves, and because Danny's father, a well-to-do businessman, had kept all four of them from starvation. Then the break: three minutes on a television programme, a documentary about housing problems in north-east London. A recording with a small company followed; a song, 'Hopeless Fool', that had been played on the radio and caught on sufficiently to scrape into the Top Thirty. After that the big contract, the song that was a real hit, 'Like Us'. It had taken them, for a whole month, to number one in the charts.

They'd never had such a success again, and in many ways Aaron was relieved. Life at the time had been so frenetic that the pace could never have been sustained: the nightly appearances, the constant travelling, the rapturous fans. And the money. He'd gone mad, spending wildly. But hard drugs, at least, he'd avoided, and when Dominic smashed up, completely wrote off, an almost brand-new car in which Aaron was a passenger, and from which they both escaped without a scratch, he sobered up. The money went into the bank and, eventually, the cottage. The Greenwich house he was buying on a mortgage; hence the need for tenants. "I don't work twenty-four hours a day at being Aaron Brown any more," he told a newspaper reporter. "Just twenty-three." But he still lived for the one hour he spent on the stage every night. "It's sheer magic," he said in the same interview, then added, bitterly, "I had a woman for three years but I've lost her now. There wasn't time for anyone: it's crazy; now that she's gone, there is. It was a choice. At that stage in my life I either had a deep, meaningful

relationship or a career in rock music. I couldn't have both. Then."
He was talking of Lynwyn, the coloured girl he'd lived with when
he first moved to London. Later she returned, but it did not last: too
much damage had been done. So, two promiscuous years, then,
eventually, Cheryl. It was she who had given him back the private
life he'd lost; and, if he hadn't found it then, he was certain he
would have cracked up, disintegrated completely.

His appeal as a singer came partly from his total belief in what he
was doing, and partly from an innate instinct for using his natural
sexiness. He was tall and slim, and at the same time arrogant, sulky:
very attractive but seemingly unavailable. The girls, when asked,
invariably said it was his hair: shoulder-length curls of an almost
bleached colour like a Scandinavian's. It was certainly the most
immediately striking attribute of his appearance. The decline of the
group's popularity coincided, was perhaps to some extent
occasioned, by a change in his image. Though still very sleek at
twenty-four, he had put on weight; his hair was cut shorter, and he
had grown a long droopy moustache. He didn't care; he was
enjoying the greater freedom he had now he was less in demand.
The group's career was far from finished; there were enough gigs,
and they still made singles and albums that sold, that kept a more
than reasonable supply of cash flowing. In a year or two, of course,
it might be all over. He didn't think much about that. There was no
chance of enduring fame like Mick Jagger's, no likelihood of a
second career as a general entertainer, a Tommy Steele: he lacked
the personality. But he'd had a ball, much more than is allowed to
most people of his age: travel, money, and so many girls he'd lost
count. At least there was no need now for tranquillisers. And there
must be much more in himself, he was sure, left to discover.

He didn't mind Jack being at the cottage. He liked his gay
tenants (certainly they were preferable to Luke, with his
insufferable intellectual superiority) and the ménage worked, he
felt, *because* they were gay. If they'd been women, or if it had been a
bloke and his girlfriend, there would have been tensions, and,
worse, probably, female friends of theirs in droves, waiting to
goggle at him and waste his time. He'd trusted Jack and Kevin not
to broadcast to the world the identity of their landlord, and they
had not done so. The house at Greenwich mercifully had few unwanted callers, and girls who knocked on the door, hoping for a
glimpse, were disappointed. He simply never opened it if he was

31

alone, and Cheryl always did so if she was there. She had developed a good line in giving intruders the cold shoulder, despite some mistakes: the glamorous young Labour party canvasser did not perhaps deserve the reception she got. Kevin was expert, however, at coming to Cheryl's rescue. "My *dear,* he's with a *huge* black man," he once told a group of fans who had burst uninvited into the hall and would not leave. "He won't be fit for *anything* for at least two weeks!" The fans had turned and fled.

Cheryl tried to persuade Jack to stay. She had read the situation correctly, and made him go out and phone Kevin – a personal call, to avoid wasting money – dispatching him to the nearest pub to obtain sufficient 10p pieces. When he returned she said, "I hope you feel better now. How is he?"

"Fine. Fine! No trouble getting through. He was in the students' common room. He's . . . thoroughly enjoying himself."

Cheryl laughed. "You sound as if you're not too happy about that!"

"No, no. Well . . . I don't think he's pining to come home."

"Good. There'd be no point in his going if he was. Now, honestly, would there?"

"He's met a sexy butch Frog," Aaron said. "Voulez-vous coucher avec moi ce soir?"

"They're more polite than that," Cheryl remarked. "They say, 'Vous permettez?' "

"How do *you* know?" Aaron raised an eyebrow, then turned on the television.

"I've heard." Jack frowned. "There's nothing wrong, surely?" Cheryl asked him.

"No. Well, if you must know, and it's probably my imagination and the line was very bad . . . he didn't seem all that pleased to hear me. He said the right things, I suppose, but . . . as if he was in a hurry or something."

"Maybe he was. Ah, you're imagining it."

"Maybe."

"The telephone's not the best way of saying 'I love you'."

"No. It isn't."

She squeezed his hand. "I shouldn't have made you ring. But I thought it was for the best."

"It's ok. My imagination, as I said."

"Bloody Proms." Aaron was fiddling with the television knobs.

"Wait!" Cheryl cried. "That's Luke!"

"So it is." They stared at the screen. There he was, arms resting on the shoulders of a dark-haired man, a look of profound concentration on his face. "Far out," Aaron mocked. "Like a teenybopper at a gig."

The piece ended (the Mozart twenty-third piano concerto, though I'm the only one of us three, Jack said to himself, who knows that): the applause, as usual, was sensational; the pianist bowed, left the auditorium, returned, and for a brief moment, the camera, panning in on the audience, held Luke in close-up: unkempt hair and sweaty skin, old dirty tee-shirt. He was clapping as wildly as anyone; delight, intense pleasure exuded from him. And I'm the only one of us three, Jack thought, who knows about the dark-haired man.

"You'd think he was in mid-orgasm," Aaron said.

Cheryl laughed. "You're still jealous."

He grunted. "I'm not."

"Wary then."

"Why should I be wary of him?"

"You are."

"Jack, who's that man he's with?"

"His flat-mate."

Cheryl, curious, said, "I didn't know he had a flat-mate."

"Yes. He's called John. He's a potter. Funny how all these intellectual left-wing socialists of working-class origin end up with middle-class artists from Hampstead or Kensington."

"What do you mean, end up with?"

"Nothing."

"Don't tell me he's joined your lot!"

"Look at that girl standing next to him!" Aaron said. "Her boobs are too big. Grotesque!"

"Since when did you complain of boobs being too big?"

In answer he grabbed at hers; she shrieked, and hit him over the head. A second later she was on her back, her arms pinned to the floor. "Shall I leave?" Jack asked, politely.

"No," Aaron said. "But change the television over. I can't stand that bloody row." It was the opening bars of Shostakovitch's *Leningrad* symphony. Jack did so; Luke and John vanished, and in their place came the Prime Minister threatening the country with more public-spending cuts.

Aaron let Cheryl go, and she stood, dusting herself down. "I wonder if Luke *will* come to the wedding," she said.

"Not if he has any sense," Aaron answered.

"When is this event?" Jack demanded. "The social coup of the year, the most impressive fixture of the autumn season, and no one knows when or where it's to be held."

"Fixture! It's not Exeter City versus Plymouth Argyle."

"All a matter of balls, perhaps?"

Aaron groaned, then laughed. "Not bad," he said. "I suppose."

"November the fifth," Cheryl announced. "Very appropriate. We've only just settled the arrangements, today. Okehampton parish church, where they've just installed a new central-heating system, and the bride will wear white."

"I see," said Jack. "The registry office isn't good enough for you."

"No. It's to be a proper job, as they say down here, and a deadly secret because we don't want the press. The vicar's sworn to silence on pain of instant crucifixion, and so are Mum and Dad, and Ron's parents, and his nine-hundred-and-three brothers and their wives-stroke-girlfriends, and you."

"An awful lot of calvaries in England's green and pleasant land."

"I've three brothers," Ron said. "And they're all happily married. As far as I know."

"You're to be invited, Jack," Cheryl went on. "And Kevin. And the rest of Aaron's Rod and their molls, and Tim and Ray who are two friends of Ron's, and four girls I know, Luke, and innumerable aunts, uncles, cousins and grandparents on both sides. A small wedding."

"Who's the best man?"

"Ray Suñer," Aaron said. "I was at school with him. Oh, you'd like him, Jack. One of your crowd. And so is Tim Keegan."

"You know rather a lot of gays, Ron. You rouse my darkest suspicions."

"So it's all decided," Cheryl said. "Now to more important matters. Are you staying, or rushing off to Liverpool?"

"Staying."

"Right. So, this evening's plans: we're all three of us going back to the farm to have dinner with my parents. Ok?"

"Great."

"And I do not know a lot of gays," Aaron added, almost as a footnote.

"You do."
"Four. It's a coincidence."

A message one morning, written in red crayon on a mirror:
"Look in tub with yellow dahlia." Tied to this ailing specimen was,
"I can't say I'll live with you and love you till death do us part. I
can't say I'll never sleep with someone else, man or woman. Look
in bath." There lay a postcard of a Bonnard nude, also in a bath; on
the back these words: "Love me. Trust me. Above all, help me."
John replied, on a print of Botticelli's *Primavera*: "Your letters are
receiving attention. In answer to the three instructions in your last
communication, a) I admit nothing, b) I do, and c) short of
throwing myself under a bus, I'll do anything you ask."

Chapter Three

The Mini was off the road due to a combination of various troubles:
the bottom hose of the radiator had worn out; the exhaust pipe was
broken, and the whole car shuddered all the time it was being
driven. A loose prop shaft, Luke thought.

"Why don't you just throw it away for scrap?" John asked.

"And have nothing left to travel about in."

"There's mine. We use it more than yours, anyway." The idea
was eminently sensible, but Luke dismissed it out of hand. To
abandon his car altogether was to sacrifice his most visible sign of
independence; he was not ready to do so. John knew this, so did
not press the point, except to comment about the unnecessary
money it swallowed up. "The cost of running that sardine tin means
gallons to the mile, not miles to the gallon," he grumbled.

"Piss off!" But he was right, of course; and after thinking about it
for a week Luke went out one Saturday morning and sold it for a
hundred and thirty pounds. He had not thought he was the kind of
person who had a sentimental attachment to cars; they were
simply objects that were useful for transporting him from A to B,
even if driving John's Dolomite was a lot nicer than steering the
Mini. But parting with it was not easy. It was more than just a
symbol of his freedom that was being surrendered; the car was
inextricably bound up with the three or four most interesting years
of his life. It was the only thing of his brother's he possessed. As he
pocketed the money he wondered if Adam, across the other side of
the world in Brisbane, shivered and thought someone was treading
on his grave. There were other memories: at the age of seventeen
he'd made love to Elaine Stephens on the back seat, the day after

he'd passed his driving test. Dreadfully uncomfortable, elbows and heads banging metal. It had been vital that snowy freezing weekend when his father had died, and later he and Cheryl had been all over the country in it. He went home by bus, staring gloomily at the Saturday shoppers in Notting Hill Gate hurrying from one store to the next to escape the pouring rain. The hiss of tyres on the wet road reminded him of the traffic ploughing through the slush that Saturday he'd waited for Cheryl in the Tartan Café, and gone out with her to find her lost horse. He was no longer in charge of his own destiny, he thought. What was this John to him that he should be persuaded into giving up his car?

"Hullo."

He turned round, and for a split second did not recognise the girl in the seat behind, just registered the young face, slightly flushed and wet with rain, the dark eyes sparkling. "Cheryl!"

"Don't sound so amazed! It was always quite possible we'd bump into each other. Surprising we haven't, with you coming over to see Jack and Kevin."

"I'm sorry; I was miles away. I've just sold the Mini, and I was beginning to regret it."

"The times I've cursed that bloody old heap breaking down on us! I could never understand why you were so attached to it."

She wiped a strand of wet hair away from her eyes. He winced at her words; still trying to hurt him even now, he thought. Why doesn't she forgive and forget? "How are you, anyway?" he asked.

"Me? Fine. I'm getting married."

"Married! Who to?"

She burst out laughing. "Who do you think?"

"Aaron?" He stared in disbelief. Aaron!! Whenever he'd thought about it, which wasn't very often, he always imagined she'd moved in with her old landlord because it was the obvious thing to do at the time; any other option was so hard. Aaron meant money, security, not having to find somewhere else to live. She would not have decided in such a calculating cold-blooded way, of course; no, that would be to impute to her base motives that she was incapable of considering, but, at a subconscious level, he had thought such forces she'd find difficult to resist. She presumably found Aaron physically attractive and interesting enough as a person and in his lifestyle, but he'd assumed, for no good reason, that it would be a strictly temporary arrangement. Cheryl *marrying* Aaron! She deserved better. If ever there was a self-centred narcissistic pig, a born wanker, it was Aaron!

His prolonged scrutiny made her blush; she looked out of the window. "Well, congratulations," he said, trying to sound pleased, but knowing that his voice was full of dismay. She did not answer. "Where are you going?"

"High Street Ken."

"So am I." A change of mind; he had intended, as he was returning to the flat, to get off at the Albert Memorial, but this piece of news deserved more than a few brief words on a 52 bus. "Let's have a drink to celebrate. It's half past twelve, drinks time anyway."

"I'm in a bit of a hurry."

"Please. Just a quick one."

"Oh, all right."

They went into the Catherine Wheel. He drank lager, she a sweet Martini. "Our tastes in alcohol don't change," he observed. "When's it to be, this wedding?"

"November the fifth at Okehampton. Mum will be sending you a card."

"I'm invited?"

"Naturally."

"Your parents. Not you."

She ignored that, and said, "We saw you on telly a few weeks back. A prom, Mozart or somebody. You were with a friend."

"John. We share a flat."

"*Will* you come to the wedding?"

He squinted into his beer, swilled it round in the glass. "Might be a bit embarrassing."

"And Luke never likes being embarrassed." She sounded so hostile that he looked up. She was attractive in the way she was when he first knew her; gone was the cow-like adoration that used to annoy him so much, the pleading in the eyes that said I'm-suffering-and-you're-causing-it-but-I'll-put-up-with-it that tore at his conscience and dried up his feelings. She was adult and self-possessed now.

"No," he said, more to himself than to her. To cover up the pause in the conversation, he asked, "How is it I never see you when I come over to Greenwich? Do you keep out of the way on purpose?"

"Yes. They're very considerate; they tell me if you're expected."

"Kevin I suppose. Jack's not so . . . precise."

She finished her drink. "I must be going."

"Cheryl . . . are you doing the right thing?"

She stood up, pretending to look for something in her coat pocket, and said, "It's none of your business. Particularly none of your business, Luke."

"I know that. If you ever need me, any help – "

"I won't."

" – you know where I live."

"I don't."

"Look up John Perry in the phone book."

"I'm not going to say yes to ease your conscience."

"More than two years of our lives. Mostly good, some of it marvellous. You know that. You can't just chuck it away."

"You did."

"I know that."

"And now you regret it."

"No. No, I don't. Cheryl . . . there's something I ought to tell you."

"What?"

"John Perry is my lover."

"WHAT!" He wasn't joking, either; the intensity in his face she recognized from many a past experience. Luke! It wasn't possible. Luke!! "No," she said. "No. It can't be true. It *can't* be!"

"I ought to go." He looked at his watch.

"You'd better bring him to the wedding, then. Join the fucking club! That will make six of you. Talk about getting in every-bloody-where."

"Cheryl . . . please . . . " He turned and left her. She watched him walk up the street in the rain; it was a cool gusty day, but as usual he was not bothered by the weather. Old jeans and tee-shirt clinging to his body like a skin. THE ANSWER'S NO (But Keep on Trying) were the words printed on this particular tee-shirt, black on a peculiarly bilious shade of green. For a moment she thought of him in different clothes; various fragments of the past: the firm safety of his arms round her at a disco; the strong hands covered with grease, manipulating some nut in the car engine; his movements on the squash court, his legs, firm, all thick dark hair and muscle. The smile, amused, or just content that she existed, or full of desire. In bed he had really been there with her; it was with one hundred per cent of himself, thought, emotions, instincts : totally. She was sure of that. And now he was the lover of a *man*? Impossible. Her world seemed to be breaking apart at the centre. For a moment she experienced a terrible sense of panic; of course she was doing the wrong thing, marrying Aaron. Luke, come back! She shook her head, turned in the other direction, and walked towards the tube station.

"We've been invited to a wedding," he told John when he returned.

"Oh? Whose?"

"Cheryl's. We're not going, of course." He sounded belligerent. "What are you laughing at?"

"There's no need to take it out on me. We're not going, you said, so we're not going."

"Do you want to then?"

"Not particularly."

"What do you mean anyway, taking what out on you? Do you think I still fancy her?"

"Do you?"

"No." He went into the kitchen and made himself some lunch: bread and cheese and a glass of milk. "What's the programme tonight?"

"I can't, Luke; I have to work. I've a delivery next Friday to Attention, and I'm all behind."

"What absurd names your shops have! They're all abstract nouns beginning with A! Attention in Islington, Affinity in Lewisham, Activity in Hackney. Who the hell wants to buy pots in Hackney? Did you know Harold Pinter went to school there? Activity! Sounds more like a brand of trendy knickers."

"Is it knickers to this or do you like it?" John came into the kitchen, holding a piece of pottery. It looked like a giant mushroom on a huge stalk about two feet long, beautifully glazed, black and gold on oatmeal.

"Modelled on me I suppose," Luke said, his mouth full of cheese. "Just your size."

"You get more and more coarse. Once upon a time it was all poetry; now it's crude rhymes and sexual innuendos in everything."

"What do you expect, you make potted phallic symbols! How many have you sold?"

"They're *not* phallic symbols. And they're selling very well."

"I'm not surprised. What are they for?"

"They're not *for* anything. I've explained more than once" – John sounded weary – "that pottery isn't just utilitarian; it isn't all mugs and cruets. The best part is inventing something new."

"Uh-huh. You make some more then. I do like it, actually."

"Good. What will you do this evening?"

"Go and see Jack, I think. Kevin's home now, or should be. It's only the Viennese night and I don't want to hear that. A game of squash and a few pints; I'm in a drinking mood. Why not give Cheryl one of those as a wedding present?"

"Don't be ridiculous. I *would* like to go to the wedding, though. I can see where you come from then. Your roots. Are you sure I was invited too?"

"Council houses look much the same in Okehampton as they do in Kensington. And no, I'm not sure you were invited too." He put his arms round John and kissed him. "I ran into Cheryl on the bus this morning, and she told me. That she was getting married, I mean. It took a few moments to adjust; I mean . . . . it's as if I had a sister, in a way."

"And have you adjusted?"

"Soon as I got back here and saw you. Come into the bedroom and I'll prove it."

"I have to go out."

"Yes, yes. 'Had we but World enough and Time, This coyness Lady were no crime.' You wanted poetry, you said."

"And was Cheryl poetic?"

"No. Bloody rude, as a matter of fact. I told her about . . . . us."

"Oh. I see."

Cheryl, exhausted from her morning's attempt at shopping, trying on clothes all over town and finding none to her liking, took off her shoes and lay on the sofa, drinking coffee. Aaron she had expected to be in, but he was not. Bloody men. Luke, Aaron, just the same. Luke was marginally worse. No, considerably worse. All they wanted was mothering and a receptacle in which to shoot their seed, gay, straight, bi, the whole sodding lot of them. Why was

Kevin so much nicer, and, irony of ironies, quite out of the question?

John concentrated on the clay. They were going to be excellent, these toadstools. He could sense it in his fingers. That afternoon had been the best ever with Luke; for minutes, it seemed, collision, collision, collision. But all the same he knew Luke wasn't totally disconnected from Cheryl. Did it matter? Now his lover would be sweating buckets on the squash court, and soon he'd be filling himself with beer. His animal energy was extraordinary, a joy to see and experience. I love him, love him, love him, love him, love him! But I'll never tell him that.

"Look, I know I should beat you," Luke said as he ordered the first round in the Yacht, "but that was ridiculous. What's the matter with you? And where's Kevin? I thought he'd meet us here as usual."

"He's in Chester."

"What on earth is he doing there?"

"A long story."

Jack fiddled with an ash-tray. He looks positively ill, Luke thought. Something was wrong, seriously wrong. "You'd better tell me," he said.

Kevin had met someone at Montpellier, another man on the course, and had gone to stay with him for a few days. Perhaps it was more than just a change, he'd admitted to Jack, but nothing of any significance, nothing that would interfere with their relationship. Yet he'd been on the phone to this Toby almost every day since he'd returned, and talked of the possibility of moving out, finding a room of his own. No, he didn't want things to finish with Jack, but their life together had not been a success just recently. Of course they would go on seeing each other and share the same bed most nights; why not? *And* cook his meals. He never ate properly if someone didn't cook for him. In a rage Jack smashed a record, an old 78 of Piaf singing 'La Vie en Rose', their record, *their* tune. Kevin was dreadfully upset, had clung to him, grieved at the loss. And, later, when Jack had gone out without saying where and not returned for three hours, Kevin wept. "I thought you'd been killed in an accident!" he sobbed. "And I was thinking, if it was Toby and not you, I wouldn't feel anything!"

"I'd knock his teeth in," Luke said.

"Whatever would be the use of that?" Jack asked. He could see Kevin's point of view only too well. The grass is always greener. He, too, wanted other men from time to time, though he would never leave Kevin for days on end, not even for a single night. Sleeping alone was utterly intolerable! Waking from bad dreams to find the other half of the bed empty, hours of sleeplessness. "Every man wants a secure loving long-term commitment," he said. "You know that as well as I do. And at the same time, the freedom to act on the spur of the moment, regardless of responsibilities to his partner. Straight or gay, equally alike."

"If you deliver ultimatums," Luke said, "the worst results will occur. Tell him to fuck off and he will. Order him to come back one to one as you were, and he might, but oh how unwillingly! It sounds hard, Jack. You'll just have to let him work it out for himself; sit by and suffer and hope."

Kevin insisted on phoning each day, salving conscience presumably. Not to pick up the receiver was more than Jack could stand. I love you, Kevin always said; it's all right. I'll be home. But Jack was reduced to an incoherent stammer, said all the wrong things, such as did you have sex last night; was it good? He was rapidly becoming an exhausted wreck, not eating, smoking too much, his bowels in a constant state of diarrhoea, stomach churning with emotion all day and all night. To lie awake, thinking of his lover in someone else's arms, in satisfied sleep, or maybe even at that moment . . . In one conversation Kevin had said they were thinking of going to Gloucester. He wanted to take Toby round the cathedral, and introduce him to his parents. That was the unkindest thing of all: yes, Jack could well imagine the over-indulgent, supposedly tolerant Sullivans accepting Toby just as they'd accepted Jack, Mr Sullivan bringing out the bottles, himself relegated in their minds to the status of ex-boyfriend, no questions asked, washing their hands of it, splendid replicas of Pontius Pilate! Out of sight, out of mind : that was the Sullivans' code of behaviour, their conscious morality. Jack detested Kevin's parents: their desire to be liked and looked up to, their phoney liberalism that masked disapproval almost as strong as his own father's, sickened him. At least with Mr Crawley there was no hypocrisy.

"Doesn't he *know* what he's doing?" Luke asked. "Doesn't he realise how he's tearing you up?"

43

"No. I'm sure of that. I really don't think he has any idea. He's convinced himself he's just having a good time, no strings attached, and that I ought to be doing the same thing. And we did agree we needed a break from each other. Though this . . . it never occurred to me! How naive can you get!! The worst moment . . . I took him out to dinner, two days after he came back from France. I thought a good evening out, a meal . . . he'd realise, wake, as it were, from a dream. He looked round the flat when we came in, and said 'I hate this place'. All our shared things . . . 'I hate this place'."

He gripped the edge of the table. Luke stood up, and pulled him to his feet. "Come on," he said. "You're coming back with me. Now! You're not going to the flat, not by yourself, not till Kevin's home. We can make up the sofa into a bed, or if you really can't sleep alone, you can climb in with us."

They went outside, to Jack's car. "Will you drive, Luke? I . . . don't think . . . " Luke put an arm round him, and let him cry. "I don't know what I'd do if he left me! I . . . could —"

"He won't leave you."

"He might well . . . I just couldn't go on living!"

"Yes, you will." He stroked Jack's hair: Jack was shaking, uncontrollably.

"I'd be dead inside! Do you understand me? Shit! Have you got a handkerchief?"

"Here." Luke passed it over. "I haven't . . . ever given myself like that. Perhaps I've been too frightened. My mother, then Dad: their dying jammed up a lot inside me. I said to Cheryl once I'd never love like they did. Never! The hurt to him when she died! All I've done, I've got to admit, is hurt other people. Cheryl. I don't mean to, but . . . Jack, I envy you. Loving like that. Do you know I still find myself thinking when I've done something worthwhile, something interesting, that I must tell Dad about it, and then saying, I can't, he's dead . . . yes, sometimes very bitterly, *the bastard* dying on me like that!"

"You gave him a lot of love."

"Maybe." He was silent for a moment, then said, "What about Kevin?"

"What about Kevin?"

"Does he . . . did he . . . really love you?"

"More than I loved him, or so I always thought till now, till I'm

44

about to lose him, and know, yes, too late, how much I do love him. Yes, I think I was his entire world. I couldn't always cope with that. In a gilded cage . . . I'd accuse him of being possessive, neurotic. Perhaps I just didn't appreciate what it was he was offering me. Perhaps that's why all this has happened. And now that I do know, it's too fucking late!''

Luke started the engine. They drove home in silence. John was out, presumably still at the pottery; he had left a note in the hall: ''There's a letter for you on the mantelpiece – the postman delivered it downstairs by mistake.'' It was from a newspaper Luke had written to so long ago he'd forgotten they had never replied. The *Minehead Weekly News,* in darkest Somerset. They liked the sample of work he had sent them, and they had a vacancy for a reporter, a young man who had drive, energy, ambition, and, they added, a capacity for fitting in well with other people. Would he care to go down and see them? It would be useful if he had a car: the area they covered was enormous and included the Brendons, the Quantocks, the whole of Exmoor. He was stunned. Delighted beyond measure! John? Yet it took only a moment for him to decide that if he was offered the job he would accept it.

It was not the time now to think about that, however. Jack was the first priority. Luke opened a bottle of John's whisky. ''A small one?'' he asked. ''Or do you want to get drunk?''

''I don't care.''

I can come back every weekend, he thought, hitch-hike or something. Or he can come down. Jack was talking, and he wasn't even listening! How easy it was, how appallingly easy that in one single moment he could put John out of his head and then Jack, at the worst crisis of his life! Was he really so ungenerous, so selfish? ''Does Cheryl know what's happening?'' he asked, trying to find the correct place in Jack's words.

''I haven't said. I will, I suppose . . . but I don't want to worry her. Her mind's full of wedding plans. I wouldn't tell Ron, face to face . . . I mean, I can see little point. Luke . . . I don't think I'll have a whisky. Is coffee ok?''

''Instant only. It deliquesces. Lovely word.''

But Jack, after so many broken nights and having at last shared his problems, fell asleep before the water boiled. Luke explained to John when he came in. He had no objection to Jack staying for a few days.

45

"What was your letter about?" he asked.

"Oh . . . just a newspaper." John nodded, assuming this meant another rejection. It was too late at night, Luke decided, to go into the matter. But he lay awake for some time, thinking about it. Was it a quirk of personality, he wondered, or some characteristic of the lifestyle of his entire generation that made people behave, in their relationships, so selfishly? His was the first generation in history that had been able to live a satisfactory sex-life from adolescence onwards. They were free of the pressures of religion, of begetting unwanted children, of the disapproval of their elders. Their elders, in fact, occasionally seemed to think it almost mandatory that the young should leap into bed with one another, to compensate, perhaps, for their own pre-marital frustrations. Few frowns were directed at boy and girl living together, and censure when couples parted or found new partners was mild. Censure, of course, continued to be directed at the kind of relationship he had now. Many reasons for that, he supposed; a feeling that making love with your own sex was an inferior experience (the plumbing didn't match), or that homosexuality was contagious like a disease, or sterile in that it didn't reproduce the species and therefore evaded responsibilities. But what you did in bed was probably the most fundamental cause of censure. A cock shoved up an arse. Filthy, disgusting, the world said. Ridiculous! As for two women in bed : well, that drove heterosexual men crazy with frustration, fear, and hatred. They seemed to diminish the male, those women who didn't need a man; made him feel useless.

He had never had such fears himself. Even when he had considered that he was completely heterosexual, he had on no occasion thought gay relationships inferior or wrong. Maybe, he thought, that was because he was in part homosexual but had not known it then. Had he been born thirty years previously, that side of him might never have surfaced: sure, he could well have lost his virginity, as he had done, at sixteen, to a girl (naturally), but at twenty-one he'd probably be still with her, engaged to be married, saving up to buy a house. The temptations of sleeping around would have been easier to resist when contraception was less reliable, and living together without promises would have been unthinkable.

John. Was this the one really mature relationship most people were allowed once in a lifetime? A man : that was the extraordinary thing. Most bisexuals, he assumed, would opt in the end for a woman, marriage; there would be children and society's approval : it was an easier road. The desire for men could be satisfied with a quick screw when the wife wasn't looking. Would he be the same, ten years hence? Impossible to know the answer. For the moment, it was John : with him there was some kind of rhythm in which two people danced in mutual harmony, distancing, coming together, allowing the space each wanted mentally and emotionally, yet bound, because they could not envisage – despite John's taunts that Luke would leave him – a probable end to it, an easy move to another mode of existence next week or next month. Or even next year. One did not lightly sacrifice something like that. The challenge was to keep it, develop it further, in a new context, nearly two hundred miles apart. What did it involve? Sexual fidelity? Making a set of rules for each other? Try Somerset, and if things went wrong between them, give it up? Make John move down with him? No. None of these would work.

Just go on being themselves, giving to each other as they had done. And hope. He did not look forward, however, to explaining all this in the morning, nor was it likely John would think of it in exactly the same way that he did.

Aaron had a week of gigs in the West Country, and Cheryl decided to meet him at the cottage on the Friday night so that they could have the days together. She went to see the group perform, at a crowded noisy club in Exeter. Aaron's Rod was tired and stale, she thought; it was time they had a long break, a much-needed rest, and seriously considered their future. Packed though the club was, it was a curiously respectful audience. There were no ecstatic girls; people either concentrated on their dancing or listened to the music. It was as if the group's style had passed into the world of yesterday. Their newest song, 'Can you Boogie?', which Aaron had been plugging for all he was worth, was too close to 'Like Us' of four years ago. He went through his act as a very passable imitation of when he was the youthful idol in the number-one slot; he could still flick his fingers, wiggle his hips and jerk his guitar as suggestively as ever: the bulge in his tight jeans constantly offered a sweet promise that was tantalising, though no one ran forward now to touch the hem of his garment or pull down his zip. He looked as if he'd been there too long, done too much. As was indeed the truth,

47

more or less. And the moustache was absurd.

Afterwards Cheryl discovered him in an office back-stage, lying on a sofa, the rest of the group and a dozen other people crowded round him. A girl pressed a glass of water to his lips. He looked ashen.

She pushed her way through. "What's happened?" she cried.

"Nothing. I passed out, that's all." He touched her face. His hand, clammy with sweat, was cold.

"Passed out! How? Has someone sent for a doctor?"

"He's on his way," Kenny said.

"Fuss about nothing," Aaron grumbled. "Anyone can faint."

"You said one leg had gone numb."

"Yes, well, it had. But I feel better now."

"Numb!" Cheryl was horrified. "Ron . . . what is it?"

"My right leg just felt . . . as if it wasn't mine. As if it couldn't support me any longer."

"What dope's he had?" someone asked.

"Only a joint. Well, so what if I did?" He looked at the others. "We all did! It hasn't bothered Danny or Guy or Dominic."

The doctor came. His verdict was a relief: tiredness, too much strain. A complete rest was the only answer. Out of the question, Aaron said; they had Plymouth tomorrow night. And five engagements next week. "Up to you," the doctor answered. "Perhaps your girlfriend can knock some sense into you."

"I will," Cheryl said grimly. "Don't worry."

"If he doesn't rest, I wouldn't like to say what might happen."

"Bollocks," Aaron said, when the man had gone. Cheryl took him out to the car. He was walking with a pronounced limp in his right leg. "See you in Plymouth," he said to Danny. "Seven o'clock. Can you clear up here?"

"We'll come out to the cottage at tea-time," Danny answered.

"No you bloody won't!"

"Don't be such a fool, Ron," he said, patiently. Aaron looked at him, then got into the car. Cheryl drove.

Later, at the cottage, he emerged from an almost unpleasantly hot shower, and sat on the edge of the bath. Cheryl dried his legs. "What was it, do you think?" she asked.

He ruffled her hair. "Nothing."

'I'm worried." She buried her face against him.

"Hey!" He laughed. "We'll see if anything's wrong with that,

48

shall we?" In first-class working order, he said later; not all of him needed a twelve-thousand-mile service.

In the morning they walked along the estuary to the Turf Inn. It was a bright squally day, the wind wrinkling the water into glittering clusters of fleeting brilliance. The white boats of summer had all gone. Perhaps it was the wind that made progress difficult, but Cheryl thought that Aaron was still limping slightly. They crossed over the lock-gates, and were glad of the warmth of the pub. They were the only drinkers: they sat in front of an open log fire, silent, listening to the gale dance in the chimney, to the window-frames struggle and knock as the wind tried to smash in the glass. Outside, the river, now dull-coloured as cloud pulled across the sun, flickered uneasily. An old half-submerged hulk quietly rotted against the shore; that and the outlines of Exmouth across the water were the only things static in a rushing landscape.

The rest of the group arrived in the afternoon and an argument developed; they and Kenny and Cheryl against Aaron, who got his own way of course. Cheryl said she would come to Plymouth that evening. She had intended to drive to Okehampton to see her parents, but phoned them to cancel the arrangement. Mr Wood said he couldn't understand why she was so insistent that they should come to the club in Plymouth instead: hardly their scene.

Aaron collapsed on the stage, three-quarters of the way through his act. There was a tremendous hullaballoo; photographers' flash-bulbs, a fist-fight as the audience pressed too close and trampled on the group's equipment. A guitar was smashed, Aaron's, his most expensive; Danny Jones was nearly arrested for punching a man on the jaw. Ron was taken to hospital, but hours later, on Mr Wood's orders, he was driven to the farm on the edge of Dartmoor.

He had suffered a mild stroke.

The group's engagements were cancelled for an indefinite period. The wedding was postponed.

Chapter Four

Soon after he came back from Chester Kevin decided to rent an attic room at the top of a house owned by an alcoholic Turk who spent most of his time arguing and fighting with his girlfriend. This man knew Kevin was gay, but he had no objection if some other male appeared downstairs with him at breakfast-time. Not that this often happened, despite the muddle of Kevin's intentions; most nights he still slept in the flat with Jack. The new digs well illustrated how confused he was: the only things he took with him were his clothes and a few pieces of crockery and cutlery; books and records and pieces of furniture which were his, or which he and Jack had acquired jointly, he left behind.

Jack found some old letters Kevin had written soon after they first met, and he made Kevin read them. "My sweetheart, I love you. But love's strange. For with me it means I want you when you're not there: I look to you when I'm downhearted: I snap at you when I'm happy: I upset you when I'm broody and moody: I'm heartless sometimes, the way I treat you, but you're so good and kind and loving, whatever I do: I LOVE YOU. This is a terrible Christmas here in Gloucester with you away from me. My God, my love, my heart is just about to burst at the moment while I'm writing this. I'm so happy about us, but so miserable being here. Our days of sunshine and happiness when every day will be summer for us, together all day and every day, they seem so far in the future it frightens me. I AM SELFISH. I want you now, for ever, to rule over, to be mine alone, to keep safe by me, never to let go, to make you happier than you've ever been. I love you, my love, so very much, I love you, I love you."

Kevin, who was putting his clothes into a suitcase, looked shocked, but he remained adamant. "I *must* go, Jack! I'll suffocate otherwise! It's been too close, too stifling . . . I'm smothered! I simply haven't existed as a person! I'm just beginning to discover who I am . . . I need space . . . to grow! Please, Jack, let me! Just let me be free, work it all out by myself. Please, Jack, let me go!!"

"I can't stop you."

"I just wish . . . I had your blessing."

"Blessing! For something that's tearing me up, that's killing me! Without you . . . life has no meaning! No point, nothing! Don't you realise? What more do you need of me, Kevin? What more?" Kevin didn't answer. "I think you ought to give me back my ring."

"Why?"

It was a bloodstone, not given in the first marvellous rush of love of the beginning, but after a year, when they had thought it likely that each other meant permanence. "Why? Why do you think?"

"I like wearing it."

"What does that matter? It's lost all significance; it's a mockery!"

"What will you do with it?"

"Chuck it in the river, just like I did with your birthday present!"

"What!" Kevin stared at him. He had given Jack a shirt on his twenty-third birthday. Not a very romantic present, but they were beyond the stage of beautiful, non-utilitarian gifts.

"I threw it off Tower Bridge."

Again Kevin looked shocked, but he said, with dignity, trying to control his emotions, "It was yours to do what you liked with."

"Give me back the ring!"

"No."

Jack punched him hard on the mouth. Kevin tottered, then subsided to the floor, a dazed expression on his face. Blood flowed from a cut lip. Jack kneeled beside him, caressing him as if he were a fragile wounded bird. "I'm sorry," he whispered. "I'm sorry. I didn't mean to, I didn't!" Kevin pushed him away, stood up, and went to the bathroom. He dabbed his swollen face. When the bleeding stopped he returned to the bedroom. Jack was sitting in a chair by the window, staring out at the garden. Kevin picked up his suitcase and walked out of the flat.

In the evening he came home and cooked a meal for the two of them. They went to a pub later and had a few beers; at closing-time Kevin made his way to the new digs. The room was damp and cheerless and smelled of dry rot. From downstairs came the sounds of the alcoholic and his girl shouting and swearing, and in the background there was loud music, monotonous and grating, Turkish maybe or Arabic. "Fuck!" he said loudly to his reflection in the mirror. He went out again, dithered and hesitated, then walked to Greenwich and climbed into bed beside Jack. They made love, so passionately that he thought Jack would split him in two.

It was term-time. Fortunately they did not teach at the same school. Jack found he was quite incapable of coping with the routine, the noise, the sea of faces in the corridors or the playground or the dining hall, the sheer hard slog of implanting French verbs into spotty adolescents. He asked for time off; for personal reasons, he said. "You look distinctly unwell," the headmaster observed, peering at him through gold-rimmed spectacles. He was a compassionate and intelligent man. He had guessed his young colleague's sexual orientation some time ago, but considered the matter irrelevant: Jack was a promising teacher. "Do you want to talk about it?"

"No sir."

"It's nothing to do with the school, is it?"

"No."

He looked relieved. "Well . . . it's very irregular, of course. But you can have a week. If you're not back the Monday after next I'll feel obliged to ask you for the whole story."

Cheryl and Aaron were still away, presumably at the cottage. Jack was surprised. He'd expected Cheryl to be home last Sunday evening; she had to work, he assumed, the next day. However, they wouldn't object to his intrusion he guessed, and he drove down to Devon. He left no message for Kevin. The uncertainty of it all was undermining him totally. He never knew if Kevin was going to stay, or whether he'd be in to cook: they inadvertently duplicated food, or sometimes, relying on each other to provide, nothing was bought; he could not tell any evening whether he would eat or not. His stomach was in a perpetual state of upset; the diarrhoea was chronic. The few nights alone were torture, quite without sleep except for a brief hour when he first went to bed or just before the alarm went off. If Kevin was with another man on these occasions he did not know. Kevin refused to answer when questioned, and though Jack last night had got up, dressed, and walked by his digs in the small hours, there was no way of finding out. Any one, or none, of the parked cars in the street could have belonged to a man who might, or might not, be with Kevin. The curtains in his window were shut and the room was in darkness.

Kevin returned to the flat that evening, and cooked for the two of them. Jack's share he eventually threw away. It was his turn to sleep alone in the double bed, an experience he found as awful as Jack had many times told him it was. He had to fight a mounting sense of panic; images kept invading his mind of Jack dead on a motorway or in hospital with multiple injuries. Serve me right, he said again and again, but that was no consolation. The next day and Jack still absent, it occurred to him that it was odd that Cheryl was also away. A plot, he thought; they were both at the cottage. That was the answer! His spirits rose; he no longer felt an appalled responsibility. He telephoned his friend in Chester, and suggested he came down for the weekend. He felt lightness, freedom; this was what he had been struggling for. Independence! A glorious uncomplicated weekend with Toby, like that previous few days, no jealousies, no irritations. They'd driven to Snowdonia and Alderly Edge, explored Chester, danced at discos, made love: no promises, no love till death do us part; just see you soon. He'd felt himself blossom with Toby, grow as a person. Nine feet tall.

He went out that evening to a gay pub and got himself picked up by the most attractive man in the bar. A real male man, he thought with mounting excitement as they drove home, even though his name was Robin. Girls would go weak at the knees. Long dark hair, long legs, a bit like . . . yes, Luke! When he undressed Kevin was not disappointed. But he was not gentle; a lover was just an object . It hurt so much there were tears in Kevin's eyes. That's promiscuity, the joys of freedom, he thought. Robin snored all night. Loudly. Kevin was very vague next morning about when they'd meet again. He made his escape as quickly as possible.

The weekend with Toby was pleasant enough, but it had lost something – zest, infectious bubbling excitement – and in one way at least it was a disaster: Kevin could not manage anything in bed.

"You're useless," Toby remarked cheerfully. "I don't know why I bother."

"I'm sorry. I don't know what's the matter."

"I do."

"What?"

"Jack. You're all twisted up about Jack."

"I'm not." But he had talked so incessantly about recent events that Toby had told him to shut up; Kevin was becoming a bore.

"I think you'd better get yourself sorted out one way or the other. There's no future for us at the moment, is there? I think I'd better not see you for a while. Till you've decided to leave him for good, that is."

"You don't mean it."

"I do." He leaned on one elbow and looked Kevin full in the face. "What game are you playing? Can't make up your mind, I suppose, whether what you'll get from me is worth more than you'll lose with him."

"It isn't something mercenary. It's not like that at all!"

"I didn't mean money, but yes, it's mercenary all right. You can't run two lovers at once. I know people who try, but it doesn't work. If you've got to have sex outside mariage, you'll have to find some other way. Not this, not what you're up to."

"It's not a question of sex!"

"Obviously, judging by your performance just now. It's a mess, Kevin. A big flop! You're all set to ruin your own life as well as Jack's and that's plain stupid. Write to me when you've left him." He got out of bed and put his clothes on.

"Toby! Please!"

"Come on, Kevin, Get your knickers on and grow up."

It was late in the evening when Jack arrived at the estuary, and the cottage was in darkness. He rattled the door: locked. Odd. They only bothered, normally, to lock up when they returned to London. He couldn't remember where Ron was supposed to be after the five nights in the West Country; he'd assumed Cheryl would be here, even if Aaron had disappeared to wherever was next on the itinerary. She hadn't been at Greenwich all week; where else would she be if not here?

He decided to go for a walk to kill time. He did not know the area well and it was pitch dark: better not leave the road. It was a cold night, very still, without a hint of wind. Somewhere in the distance an owl hooted. Otherwise nothing, a smothering blanket of darkness and silence. The road led uphill, away from the estuary; if he turned round he could see the lights of Exmouth and their reflections in the water and the blinking of solitary lamps in isolated farmhouses on the hills. Something alive, then, was left. But it was behind him, and he couldn't walk backwards. Ahead was absolute darkness like a huge hole, like being in the middle of nothing, himself a quintessential nothing, a glimpse of the Kevinless future. This is what it will be like, he told himself. He was frightened. Light, the prime work of God, to me is extinct . . . To live a life half dead, a living death . . . No Kevin, a living death: this is absence, deprivation, darkness. Death. In front of him a bird whirred up, terrifyingly loud. He could not even see its outline. Suppose it tangled with his face! He put out a hand, touched something, and cried out in fear. It was a bramble. He made himself go on. He thought of the times he had sat in lonely remote houses, the Woods' farm for instance; himself and Kevin, Luke and Cheryl, her parents, all enjoying a drink in front of a roaring winter fire: Kevin amusing everyone with some absurd anecdote, Luke pronouncing on the novels of Henry James or the chances of the England squash team, Cheryl swopping information with her mother about horses. Mr Wood, silent, sucking his pipe, enjoying it all. Outside (and he'd never considered it before) the darkness stretched for miles to the edges of the moor. It had not been horrifying then because he'd not thought of it like that; when they left the farm the car had always split the blackness with its headbeams and in minutes they'd been swooping down to the comforting lights of Okehampton, street-lamps shining in winking necklaces.

Enough, he said aloud, and turned. Exmouth was still there. He had been climbing and now the whole of the estuary was revealed, reflections making it gleam as if it was oily, emphasising depths and currents. He shivered.

The cottage was still unoccupied. What now? His parents? No. He had too many emotional problems already. To phone the Woods was such an obvious answer he couldn't imagine why he had not thought of it before. Cheryl answered, and told him what had happened to Aaron. Jack was very welcome to come over; Ron would be delighted to see him and so would her parents. She could give him the key of the cottage if he wanted it. He suddenly realised he couldn't face her father and mother. He'd never been there without Kevin. He might . . . well, break down again. Scenes of remembered happiness. Nice uncomplaining people: he couldn't inflict his troubles on them. He tried to explain this to her, but it sounded so confused he wondered if she understood at all. At

55

least she didn't seem annoyed. He rang off, then told himself he was stupid: where on earth was he going to spend the night?

Of course! Hugh! He found the number in his diary.

"Hugh? It's Jack. Jack Crawley."

There was a pause; perhaps Hugh had forgotten everything about him. Recognition: "Jack! Hullo! How are you?"

"Fine. Look . . . I'm in Devon. Can I come over?"

"Of course. Yes . . . that would be marvellous!"

A week later he returned to Greenwich. Kevin was in the flat, watching television. "Where the hell have you been?" he demanded. "I was worried out of my *mind*!"

"Devon. And you couldn't have been that worried or you would have found me."

"There's no phone at the cottage as you bloody well know!"

"You could have tried Cheryl's parents." Jack poured himself a drink. "Are we in two separate establishments or not?"

"I've stayed here all week, but I still have the other room."

"Stupid bloody unnecessary waste of money."

"It isn't just for passing trade. Jack . . . just give me a chance!"

"I'll give you a choice. You either come back here, permanently, one to one, and give that room up, or else go. For good."

"I can't ever go for good! I can't! Anyway, what do you mean? That you never want to see me again?"

"If I met you by chance on the heath or in the pub I'd say good evening. That's all."

"But . . . why? Why?"

"Because I can't bloody well stand it, that's why! What do you think! Have you been treating me properly just recently? Given me no cause for complaint?"

"I know. I know I haven't been fair to you. Jack, let me come back as a real mature lover, not the screaming neurotic you always used to complain about! I've got to leave you to find out how!"

"No."

"Why?"

"You return here now. Or go for good."

"Why!!"

"Because . . . there could be somebody else. I didn't say there was, but there could be. Oh, quite easily!"

"Who?"

"None of your business."

Kevin sagged onto the sofa, appeared almost visibly to shrink. He put his hands over his face. With a great effort of will Jack stopped himself running forwards, taking the boy in his arms and saying, "It's not true! I love you!" Kevin looked up. "If you really mean that," he said slowly, "why are you offering me the choice?"

Luke, after briefly exploring the ruins of the winding-house, sat on the grass at the top of the incline. Here one was king. The old railway track plunged down a dizzying slope, hurtled into woods; it was a ramp up which grovelling subjects could crawl to pay homage to their sovereign lord. In fact it was an old mineral line, built in the last century to transport iron ore from mining villages in the Brendon Hills to the port of Watchet. The villages had disappeared. Here one could put down roots, he decided. He thought about this and found, to his surprise, that he meant it. He'd never before considered anywhere, except John's flat, as a place he'd like to make his own. "A day of dappled sea-borne clouds," he said, and wondered if he was misquoting: it was at least three years since he'd read, with great enthusiasm, *A Portrait of the Artist as a Young Man.* An age, another age, another Luke. The clouds, high up, drifted inland from the Bristol Channel. Far off and miles below was the sea, pale blue, and the smudge of Watchet he supposed it must be, and between him and there nearly a thousand feet of land in height, falling away, opening out in clefts and combes, rounding in soft feminine hill-shapes, curved and hazy in the late autumn warmth. Behind him was rough ancient country, Exmoor. A gaunt Methodist chapel stood at a fork in the road, defying a row of windblown beeches.

Yes, like the young James Joyce, he could well use the wings of Daedalus, not for pretensions like forging the uncreated conscience of his race, but so that he could, like an eagle, swoop through the clean sharp air down to the village in the bottom. Roadwater, was it? A cottage he'd seen earlier he'd live in if he could. Ancient and hidden in clematis. For sale. Room enough for a pottery as well. But buying was impossible, as much of a pipe-dream as seeing John happy to throw clay in a studio in Roadwater.

Two months he'd been here now. A small old-fashioned weekly journal, its office looking and smelling as if nothing had changed in fifty years; and a handful of staff, all sympathetic friendly people who welcomed him as if into a family, who put him to work on almost every aspect of the paper except printing it: sub-editing, reporting, articles, lay-out, advertising. He loved it. Even just answering the phone. His own transport had been essential, and there was only one way of obtaining the money: Cheryl's father. He thought about this for a week, then finally summoned up enough courage and went down to Okehampton, a wretched nearly day-long journey on a series of buses. It was a mistake to come, he said to himself, as, depressed by memories, he walked up to the moor out of the dark little town of his childhood. There were too many people tragically lost to him, his dead parents, Adam, Cheryl, Cheryl's parents. Every inch of the place had invisible imprints of that other Luke, a civilisation long dead. He would never come here again. He had to, of course: Cheryl's wedding.

Mr and Mrs Wood were delighted to see him. It was like the days when he first knew them; he couldn't undertand it, then realised that because Cheryl was now getting married, to them seemed happy and settled, they'd been able to forgive him for leaving her. He was amazed, almost dumb with astonishment, when Mr Wood lent him enough money to pay the deposit on a second-hand car. Was glad to do so. It meant, he hinted, that Luke was no longer lost to him.

He'd found a Mini in a reasonable enough condition (at least, he thought, he'd know how to repair it) and ran up a considerable mileage. A ghost to investigate at Lynmouth, a fire at Lynton, a car-crash at Simonsbath, a play to review at Porlock, a stag hunt at Dulverton. For the first time in his life there was a little money in his pocket, though nothing to spend it on except alcohol and paying back Mr Wood. He was lonely in the evenings. He went out once or twice with a woman from the office. She was a lot older than him and unhappily married. Not that Luke was interested other than sexually; his emotions remained entirely in London. But whenever he thought of chucking in the job and returning, he dismissed the idea at once. It was the start of the only thing he'd ever wanted to do. And sexual frustration was a problem he solved, when he had to, in a public lavatory he found in Minehead. The woman from the office he didn't want to get involved with, though, he guessed, she might prove an excellent fuck.

When he told John after the interview that he'd been offered the job and had accepted it life was not exactly peaceful. He was a little surprised, however, at the extent of his lover's intransigence, though he knew he had no good reasons for surprise. John made no pleas, merely stated that it was all over between them. Luke would not take this seriously; it was merely the first broadside, unexpected perhaps, but not fatal. Of course it was not all over, he argued; he would phone every day, and come up to London every weekend. I won't be in if you do, John said. I'm baffled, Luke claimed; what do you want? This produced a torrent of words, sarcastic and wounding; did he seriously think he could be believed when he said I love you, and at the same time wanted to go and live nearly two hundred miles away? "You could come with me," Luke said. No, no. Absolutely not. John's work was in London; the contacts he had built up over the years were in London; his money came from selling his pottery in London. "You could start again," Luke said. Oh yes, and just as he'd built up the business Luke would be off to some other job, maybe even go abroad. Was he going to stay on a tin-pot provincial weekly for ever? It was hardly likely.

"What you really want," Luke said, "is for me to give up the job after a few weeks. For me to surrender, saying I can't live without you. Well, I shan't."

"Which all proves," John said triumphantly, "that we have no real basis for anything. To talk about love in these circumstances is absurd!" It was a good test, this, John decided. If Luke abandoned the job because the separation was intolerable, he'd sell up the pottery and go with him wherever he wanted. Commit, at last. He didn't say this, of course; that would be idiotic. Let Luke work it out for himself. John knew what he wanted : Luke, so much younger, didn't know anything about himself very clearly.

Luke was puzzled. Drama he expected – tears, threats, – not this hard untouchable man. He loved John the more, very nearly changed his mind. He began to voice aloud his uncertainty, but this only seemed to make his lover the more determined. John would *not* see him at the weekend, indeed any weekend. If there was a clean break it would help Luke to sort himself out. "There is nothing to sort out!" he cried. After the first week away, he hitch-hiked to London, letting himself into the flat with his key. John was not there. He went round to the pottery, but it was deserted. He returned to the flat, but John did not come in. Eventually he went to sleep, worrying about John's safety, and feeling jealous of the other man whose bed he might be sharing. By morning he was certain it had been done on purpose, that John had guessed he would arrive unannounced, and after breakfast, plagued with a splitting headache, he took the train back to Somerset.

When John returned to the flat, saw the disarranged bed and smelled Luke on the sheets, he laughed. But he expected a letter or a message, and was surprised not to find one.

He compromised on one thing : Luke could write or phone whenever he wanted. He wouldn't promise to be in at a pre-arranged hour, but he found he was staying in the flat most evenings waiting for the phone call rather than going to the pottery. And Luke phoned every day. It would have been unbearable for them both if he hadn't. However, John made it quite plain that certain subjects were taboo on the phone, checking up, for instance, on whether he had slept with another man the previous night; and what Luke got up to he couldn't care less about, in no way wanted to know.

Eight weeks now, nearly nine. Luke wondered how much longer he could stand it. He walked to the car and drove down to Roadwater. "A day of dappled sea-borne clouds," he said again. He stopped by the cottage that was up for sale. John! He ached to be with his lover. He was mad, he told himself, stark raving mad! The warmth of John's body. His head on the pillow. The shared music, books, conversation. Meals, wine. The flat. Was he looking after the plants? He'd ask tonight if they'd been watered. Absorbed in his clay. John!

But if he gave up the job, what then? No solution. Yet.

Aaron's recovery was rapid. The complete isolation of the farm was of the greatest assistance: only the bleating of sheep and the wind in the fir trees intruded from the outside world. Cheryl fended off all the people who phoned. He was not a good patient, for he had no interests of any sort except music. She went over to the cottage and brought back a guitar, an ordinary Spanish instrument, not one that he used in the group. When he realised he had not lost the strength of his fingers, his spirits soared. He played for hours on end, none of the usual stuff, but flamenco and classical pieces. At the end of a fortnight he was as fully recovered as he would ever be. His right leg dragged a little.

Luke arrived one afternoon. He had heard the news from Jack and driven over on the spur of the moment. Cheryl and Aaron were surprised to discover he was now living in Somerset; discreetly they did not enquire after John. Aaron was struggling with a prelude by Villa-Lobos. He was quite philosophical about what had happened: Aaron superstar was finished. Aaron's Rod would disband. He had been thinking about it for days, and now that he had an audience – Luke as well as Cheryl – it was time to make the announcement.

"What will you do?" Cheryl asked. She had been hoping for this moment, and at the same time dreading it.

"Go on playing the guitar and singing. It's all I *can* do, isn't it? I could give myself a year off for re-education, perhaps. Learn flamenco, learn classical music *properly*."

"How are you going to do that?"

"Don't know." He strummed a few chords, Spanish style. "Make a brief visit to Spain, I think."

"Spain."

"Uh-huh." He refused to be drawn any further. "Don't worry about the finances. There'll be a reasonable income this year, though next year . . . well . . . "

Luke and Cheryl exchanged glances. "This was our bedroom, once upon a time," Luke said. It wasn't perhaps the most delicate way of re-starting the conversation. Aaron smiled his most cat-like smile, and began to play, "Here comes the bride."

The wedding was now arranged for New Year's Eve. "And bring John with you," Cheryl said.

"Why?" Luke asked.

"You've kept him hidden away for long enough. I'd like to meet him . . . Maybe I'm curious."

"Doesn't sound like a good reason for inviting him."

Cheryl shrugged her shoulders. "Suit yourself. See if I care."

"Ok," Luke said. "I'll bring him. He did say, in fact, that he'd like to come. But . . . he may have changed his mind."

Kevin left. It was the only possible thing to do in the circumstances. He didn't believe, though, that he would never see Jack again, that they wouldn't come back together as lovers – and soon perhaps – just as he didn't believe Jack had met somebody else he loved so much and found so compatible that he would throw up his job and move down to Devon to be with him. This Hugh worked near Totnes; how could you keep a love affair alive when you were two hundred miles away? The physical distance between himself in Greenwich and Toby in Chester had meant, right from the start, that neither of them had regarded it as a very serious proposition: it was just fun. The same, he hoped, applied to Jack and Hugh.

What impelled him to go was the ultimatum: return now on Jack's terms, or depart for ever. It was impossible, the worst foundation imaginable for a continuing relationship to crawl back, defeated and humiliated, however much he was in the wrong in the first place: you give love freely, not at the point of a pistol. Oh yes, he'd have returned all right, no doubt about it, but Jack had put it out of consideration with his demands. For the moment. The one bright prospect was Cheryl's wedding. He was bound to see Jack there. Maybe then they could pick up the pieces.

He was free now, and it was much more of a real freedom than when he had first taken the room, for if Jack was rarely out of his thoughts or emotions, Kevin never actually saw him. He kept away from the flat and Jack did not try to get in touch. Cheryl he missed greatly: those comfortable sessions doing their ironing together, discussing the men they fancied, drinking endless cups of tea. He wrote to her, giving his new address, and she replied, saying she'd call round one evening. But she didn't. So, what to do with this freedom, yearned for for so long, arriving so late, this great block of time that was as difficult to handle as an awkward bulky parcel? He cooked when he pleased, or went out to eat if he didn't like his empty room; took himself to the cinema more often than he usually did. He bought new clothes, had his hair dyed blond, haunted the gay meeting-places. It was time for sleeping around. When things were not good with Jack he'd envied those friends who were unattached and wanted to stay that way, who went with whom they pleased, who slept with dozens of different people. Gay life for them was a perpetual start to things, for that often seemed to be the only good time of it, when a new boyfriend was a marvellous promise: the anticipation, the initial exploration, changed after a night or a week or a month for somebody apparently more exciting. It was an experience he thought maybe everybody needed sooner or later. It hadn't happened to him; he'd met Jack when he was only a callow boy in his first term as an undergraduate at Exeter, just out of the sixth-form of his provincial school.

Now was the time to catch up on that missed experience, and he threw himself into the attempt with enthusiasm. But though it had moments it was less than satisfactory: he was too conscious of what he'd lost. There was, it was true, no difficulty in finding someone congenial and good-looking to sleep with, though it was never Mr Right he met on the dance floor. At least it was good for morale, he told himself, a sign that he was not one of the ugly and unwanted. Different bodies, never exactly what was expected before the clothes were shed: beauty – or disappointment – that had not always been hinted at. Astonishing how the penis varied in length or thickness, was attractive or repellent. Why should the size of it matter? It didn't to lovers, but it did, apparently, in a casual pick-up. The procedure in bed was often a waste of time, sometimes fair, once or twice physically satisfying. But meaningless. He could have sex with almost anybody: it meant nothing. And nothing of it was as good as the known, familiar (and, no doubt of it, very beautiful) body of Jack, nothing so completely overwhelming as when they had made love with real passion and tenderness.

He quickly wearied of this life and began to say to himself, I've done it. I've experienced it, I know what it's like, it's time to start an affair. Why haven't I found a new lover? Jack did, first time off. Is Jack a more attractive proposition than I am? Is that it? Could be. Thinking about it was a stab of pain : he pushed his past life out of his head. Do I have some invisible notice hanging round my neck that says "Great for a one-night screw but nothing else"? Or . . . is it that I don't really want another lover? Is it? No! I do, I do! Love me, somebody, please! Anybody!

Anybody turned out to be a scruffy New Zealander called Leslie, the same age as himself. Kevin moved in with him. At least it made a change from the types he often seemed to get landed with : married men escaping from their wives for a few hours, or boys his own age pretending they weren't really gay, deluding themselves that it was somehow easier to find a man rather than a woman.

Leslie worked in a Wimpy bar. He and Kevin had nothing in common apart from an almost total tolerance of anything the other might or might not do. They shared a bed, and they had sex together except when they were busy with someone else. But each time with Leslie Kevin thought was one more step to the end; this affair – if you could call it an affair – had a finite number of orgasms: it would soon be over. It was one step nearer to Jack.

He wrote to Cheryl a second time, and one evening she came to see him. He was just about to go out, but was delighted to change his mind. She was most apologetic for not having contacted him before, but so much had been happening: Aaron's illness, the group disbanding, the cancellation of engagements, redrafting contracts and so on. She had been kept unbelievably busy; she'd felt it necessary for once to act for Ron, to take him away from the stress. She'd given up her job. They'd been for a holiday, to Spain.

Jack was well. Not happy of course; he spent much of his free time alone in the flat, and when he wasn't there he was often with Luke's friend, John. Yes, Hugh had stayed most weekends.

Cheryl took no side. There was nothing in what she said of censure or blame. She showed only pleasure at seeing Kevin, and the wish that her little household would soon be restored as it was.

"It's up to Jack," Kevin said, sadly.

"I don't know. Not necessarily."

"Well . . . we'll see. I want it; I don't need to say that, do I?"

"No." She smiled. "I could bang your heads together. The two of you eating your hearts out, separated. Is it . . . pride?"

"No. Something much more complex than that."

"Well. You'll see each other at the wedding."

"New Year's Eve. I'm so impatient for it!"

She laughed. "It's me who's getting married, not you."

"Yes. I hope you've tied yourself up properly to his money."

"You don't understand, Kevin."

"No. There's a great deal I don't understand. Me, mostly."

"We're a lot closer since he's been ill. A lot closer."

"Nursemaid. Needed."

"More complex than that, as you said just now. And we all like being needed."

"Making him feel he couldn't live without you."

"A little of that."

"They all want mothers, maids, cooks, nurses. In return they offer money, security, screwing. Then children to tie you up even further."

"Take out the children and what's so different about homosexuals? Jack's diet has suffered somewhat."

"Don't."

"Sorry. What's wrong with money, security, screwing, children? What do *you* want?"

"To be a mature adult gay man."

"Aren't you?"

"No."

"You surprise me. I thought you and Jack had everything."

"No. But we could have had. That's the pity of it."

"Come home, Kevin."

"Now?" He laughed and shook his head. "I can't just go back, any more than he could come here. We need neutral ground."

"New Year's Eve." He nodded. "Suppose it fails? You might be clutching at straws. Have you ever thought of that?"

"Of course. But . . . do you think I am?"

"It's possible."

He looked at her in some considerable alarm.

Chapter Five

Jack saw less of Hugh. There were the same problems as existed for Kevin and Toby; distance, Hugh not wanting to be drawn into someone else's nasty emotional tangles. Jack hoped for an invitation to spend Christmas at Totnes, but it did not materialise. No word, of course, had come from his parents suggesting Christmas at Okehampton, and his brother Owen had not been in contact for months. Mike and Stuart persuaded him up to Liverpool.

The view from his bedroom window at Château Garswood exactly suited his mood. It was mid-afternoon on Christmas Eve when he arrived, the light already beginning to fade. Stuart was in the bath; Mike had gone out to deliver presents across the other side of the city. Jack, left alone for a while, listened to the service from King's on the radio, and stared at the landscape. "The choristers are filling into the candlelit chapel . . ." The sky was cold and colourless. Frost stiffened the grass in the derelict field outside; rosebay willow-herb was brown and skeletal, wispy beards where flowers had bloomed barely distinguishable from the frost patterns. Beyond, to one side, was a forlorn terrace of Victorian houses, chopped off – perhaps the builder had run out of money – before it had been finished, so that its presence seemed an impertinent challenge to the countryside; and, in the opposite direction, spoiling green tree-fringed meadows, was a factory that looked as derelict as the field. There were no animals out there, no birds in the sky, no lights in the houses. It was absolutely still, and totally inhospitable. Adam lay y-bounden, y-bounden in a bond. Four thousand winters thought he not too long. Cold church architecture, cold flat landscape. The singing sublime. Downstairs the fire, tv, warm carpets, a goose for tomorrow's dinner, alcohol, tinsel: all the commercial trappings of modern merry Christmas.

It was a mistake to come, he thought. He belonged more to the landscape than the jollifications indoors. Without Kevin nothing worked: he was maimed, as if a limb had been lopped off; dead inside, without point or purpose. He acted as cheerfully as he could, not wanting to dampen Christmas for the others, but an act it was and it required effort. No amount of will-power could shake him out of this sense of frozen isolation, as if he was watching life through a plate-glass window. They realised of course; Mike said over dinner, "Don't worry, Jack. We'll give you a fabulous time." Late in the evening they went to a club in Manchester; it was the last thing Jack wanted to do, but he could not interfere with his hosts' plans. Perhaps they thought it was just what he needed; you could never tell with a club: any night you might meet the man of your dreams. You never did of course. The man of his dreams was . . . where? At home in Gloucester? Not in a gay club in Manchester, certainly. They sped down the M62, music on the car's cassette: 'Yes Sir I Can Boogie', 'When I Need You', 'Don't Give Up On Us Baby', 'Chanson d'Amour', 'Don't Cry For Me Argentina'. Nothing had hurt so much in recent months as the songs, heard unexpectedly on someone's radio or record-player, that were reminders of Kevin. They were stabs of physical pain. Once he'd sat in the back of this car with Kevin in his arms, Stuart and Mike in front just as they were now (Mike driving, Stuart feeding him cigarettes or changing the tape); it was a hot summer night at the end of his first year as a student, and they were returning to Exeter from Torquay, the dark trees of the forest on Haldon flashing by outside, Piaf singing 'La Vie en Rose' on the cassette. He'd never been so happy. That year had been such sweet pleasure, such joy that some time, somehow, there had to be a fall from grace: the gods permit only a finite quantity of happiness, and he had surely used up all his portion.

It was worse at the club than he could possibly have guessed. Not that there was anything wrong with the club itself: clean, bright, new, the music not excessively loud, the prices reasonable. But Mike and Stuart were instantly absorbed by a crowd of friends all in excited celebratory mood, and, though he was introduced, their laughter and pleasure in enjoying Christmas Eve isolated him even

67

more: what did he have to say to these strangers, nice though they seemed, on this day of all days, when lovers travelled from one end of the kingdom to the other in order to be together, when families assembled, when sons and daughters who had left home were once again sitting around their parents' fires, when Kevin was in Gloucester and he in a club in a godforsaken city a hundred and fifty miles away? What was he expected to do? Make polite conversation the rest of the night, get drunk? Single out one of these men, and after a dance or two, go off somewhere for sex? Christ!

A mounting sense of anxiety, panic, hysteria almost: if he did not get out of this tiny capsule of a club the crowds of people, the noise and intolerable heat would make him do something crazy, would utterly engulf him. He ran up the stairs and out into the cold night. Relief: what now? If they had come to Manchester in his car (it was outside the house in Liverpool where he had left it that afternoon) he would have driven it anywhere, in any direction, till it ran out of petrol. Well, what now? Walk. Too far, of course, to walk back to Mike's, and there was no one in this city he knew, not one solitary front door that would open and welcome him. Christmas Eve!

He took note of the direction, the turnings, aware that he would get hopelessly lost if he walked blindly. The pubs had shut. All Manchester seemed drunk: groups of friends shouting goodnight, happy Christmas, banging car doors; couples tipsily crossing busy roads; solitary men urinating or being sick in dark alleyways between shops. It was an exodus from the centre, a rush-hour: crowded buses and queues of cars heading for suburbs. But as time passed the vehicles pausing at red traffic lights were fewer; the pedestrians thinned out: he was mostly alone. A hot-dog stall, doing brisk business, seemed the only focal point for humanity; after that, nothing, except a prostitute shivering in a doorway, who asked him if he'd like to come inside for five minutes.

Ice on the puddles. Freezing fog. One a.m.; another hour's walking: Mike and Stuart wouldn't want to go home yet. They loved late nights. This city was not like Lowry's paintings; it was dirtier, much more drab. But perhaps by day, crowded with people, it would resemble one of those strange pictures with their toy houses and pin-men. Or perhaps not: Lowry wasn't a photographic realist, but was imposing upon the places he observed the materials of some inner vision that had only a superficial connection, Jack imagined, with the grubby reality of the city, just as his own eyes saw reflected in its pattern of decayed Victorian streets his own misery.

He returned to the club. Mike and Stuart were concerned, but, seeing his mood, asked few questions: "I had a funny five minutes," Jack said, when they asked if he was all right. "You won a prize in the draw," Mike told him, "a bottle of whisky." At Garswood, three a.m., three thirty, four a.m.: he could sleep only in snatches. He tried to read but his brain would not register the words. At last the darkness slowly dissolved, and a red dawn revealed frost. It was as if the night had burned to ash, leaving a dull, greyish thickness on things, the furred tongue of a hangover. It looked intensely cold. Even the willow-herb seemed petrified, an ancient arctic forest from which all life had departed ice ages ago.

He got up, dressed, and went out. His breath steamed. A man was trying, unsuccessfully, to start a car, shattering the dawn silence, again and again. Jack crunched through the field. The ground was rock hard; the willow-herb snapped underfoot. Spiders' webs were spinning wheels of white thread. The car revved up at last. A small piece of the sun's rim broke the horizon, and soon the whole disc emerged, thin and waterish like the last flat circle of a sweet before the tongue crushes it. Powerless, it seemed, to revive the corpse of the land, to warm anything, but its light was as normal: the frost, no longer grey ash, sparkled like the cheap tinsel indoors.

He went back to the house.

Mike was in the kitchen, making tea. "Happy Christmas," Jack said, and Mike, kissing him, said, "Next year will be better for you than this one, love."

Cheryl spent a comfortable Christmas with Aaron's family. His parents owned a pub, the King's Head. To her it was a strange alien landscape, the island in the estuary where they lived, the grey port in the distance. Flat East Anglia. "I see why you bought the cottage," she said.

He stared at her a moment, not understanding. "To remind me of the estuary? I never gave it a thought."

"Perhaps it was subconscious."

"Oh yes," he said, sarcastically.

Though she had met all the members of his family at one time or

69

another, she had never before been with them en masse. Father and four sons: fascinating to observe the differences, the similarities. Charlie, the head of the family, a slow, rural Anglo-Saxon at one with his roots, as blond and blue-eyed as Aaron; David, the eldest, not far removed from the same source despite his middle-class office job and home on a new housing estate; then Martin, the intellectual, an art teacher, the odd one out in looks being dark and brown-eyed; then Ron who had travelled the furthest, yet whose lifestyle had not really acquired any lasting mark of another but equally enduring culture, only lost that sense of belonging, unquestioningly, to a certain place; whereas Peter, the youngest, who built boats and still lived on the island, retained it intact, was nearest to his father in speech, in the cast of his mind, even in appearance: slow and a bit dull he might seem compared with his brothers, but he was easily the most sure of who he was.

Ron was the only son not yet married. At her wedding in a few days' time Cheryl would make the sixteenth member of this family. Pat, Ann and Susan were the sons' wives; Doris was the matriarch, and there were six grandchildren, all boys, two to each marriage – Wayne and Jason (David's pair), Stephen and Jamie (Martin's), and Darren and Richard (Peter's). Wayne, nearly eight, was the eldest; Jamie, at six weeks, the youngest. Peter only twenty-two, and twice a father already! He'd married at seventeen, having carelessly made Susan pregnant. Woe betide me, Cheryl thought, if I don't bring forth male children; a baby girl would be too much of a shock. The men might feel, as the males of remote peasant communities in Andalusia are said to feel, that having only daughters was a slur on their manhood.

And a chauvinist occasion this Christmas party certainly was, the sexes adhering rigidly to their traditional roles. Martin and Ann poked fun continually at the scheme of things, not from malice but because their own lives were so differently organised, were without ritual. Doris was the high priestess of the occasion, officiating in the kitchen with the rest of the women as her acolytes, or, to put it another way, Ann said to Cheryl, like some formidable cook presiding at school dinners: only the hat of office and ladles of sufficient length and number were absent. The men drank and smoked in the bar, though Martin brought a tray of drinks through to the kitchen and stayed with the women, despite Doris saying he was getting under everybody's feet. The children, apart from the

70

baby, were for once quietly absorbed; the largesse of Father Christmas (and it was, there being so many relatives, very large) was sufficient, for a few hours at least, to keep them playing happily, out of the adults' way. And after dinner it was the women who continued to work, washing up and drying dishes, while the men snored in the lounge: perhaps their take-over of official business at the table, Charlie dismembering turkey, David carving pork, Martin slicing ham, Aaron and Peter drawing corks, had exhausted them as much as the imbibing of aperitifs, wine, liqueurs, and the gorging of rich food. The children were becoming restless, and it was Pat and Susan, after the dishes were done, who supervised them, organising Happy Families and Ludo, preventing Wayne and Darren from tearing Richard in half, taking buttons and coins out of Stephen's mouth, consoling Jason who'd overwound his new plastic helicopter and broken the spring so that the blades wouldn't whirl round. Doris made tea, and as the men were still asleep, drank it with Cheryl and Ann (just as if it was three o'clock in the school kitchens, Cheryl thought), and reminisced about last Christmas when only thirteen members of the family had been present. "Most unlucky," she said. "I thought we were in for a year of it, worse than the flood year, but I was wrong it seems. Ron's fault, of course; he wouldn't come home. Always the black sheep." Cheryl, feeling guilty, blushed: last Christmas they'd spent together, alone at Greenwich. But Ann winked, and whispered, "Take no notice."

Later the women put the children to bed. Everyone was staying the night, one family to each of the four bedrooms. Aaron and Cheryl were to have the lounge sofa, somewhat to Doris's disapproval. She had originally intended that her future daughter-in-law should sleep with her ("Christ almighty!" Cheryl had said when Ron told her) and that Charlie should be booted out onto the sofa and Aaron have a camp bed in the bar; but Ron, arguing with her over the phone, said he wouldn't come back for Christmas if that was to be the arrangement: didn't she realise times had changed? For the worse, she said; no one had any morals these days. No wonder the world was in such a dreadful state. Only one of her children had had the decency to leave that sort of thing till after the wedding; where had she gone wrong, she wanted to know. Who was it, Ron asked; was there a fifth one he didn't know of? There was a pause while Doris worked that out. When she saw the joke she laughed, and said, "Well . . . I suppose it's not fair on your poor father kicking him out of his own bed and on a Christmas night into the bargain." Aaron, thinking about it afterwards, decided that Charlie might have preferred the arrangement she'd originally proposed: Doris was vast in girth and always occupied three-quarters of the mattress.

The men came to eventually, but only to pour themselves gins or whiskies and turn on the television. Everyone refused Doris's offer of cold meat and salad; later, they all said. "Peter has no appetite these days," she informed Cheryl. "I don't think Susan feeds him properly. She will go in for that spaghetti and foreign muck. He doesn't get the right vitamins."

"Are we going out?" Cheryl asked Aaron, when they had a moment alone.

He looked surprised. "Where to?"

"I don't know."

"There isn't anywhere to go. Besides" – and he glanced in the direction of the kitchen where Doris was making more tea and cutting up Christmas cake – "it won't be popular."

"A walk, perhaps, just up the road."

"All right." He was reluctant to leave the fire. "You're not bored, are you?"

"No! Not at all! Christmas with the Brown family: quite a . . . phenomenon."

"There's no need to be rude about it," he said, stiffly.

"I wasn't. I'm enjoying it. Really."

"Come on then. Let's go for this walk."

It was bitterly cold, the ground hard with frost. "Just up to the bridge and back," Cheryl said. A few flakes of snow swept in on the wind.

Aaron laughed. "I didn't think you'd go far," he said. "The night we had the flood was as cold as this."

"Tell me about it."

"Not now. It's a tale for indoors." He didn't like discussing it, she knew that; but it hurt her to think that one of the major experiences of his life he wouldn't share with her. His best friend, John Hewitt, had been drowned, and Aaron himself had only just escaped death. All the details she'd learned from other members of the family.

There was a full moon: they could see the tide flowing swiftly up the river, steadily climbing the gleaming mudbanks. It was narrower and much less interesting than the Exe, but the advance and retreat in and out of this inlet fascinated her just as much. Why was she giving herself to a man who was like this sea, she wondered, always the taker? She was the land, giving, accepting. The ground-swell could destroy: water had surged over the island seven years ago, and sometimes it eroded or ruined cliff, field, village. Yet at certain places, Wells-next-the-Sea for instance, (Aaron had taken her there once) it had receded so much that at low tide it disappeared.

Luke turned up uninvited at the flat in Kensington on the day before Christmas Eve with an expensive antique paraffin lamp and a bottle of Johnson's baby oil for presents. He found his lover, dejected and lonely, in bed reading.

"So . . . what brings you here?" John asked, propping himself up on one elbow as Luke came into the bedroom.

Luke took off his socks and sneakers, then his jeans, and said, "An insatiable and uncontrollable urge to screw you rigid."

"I see. Suppose I don't want to be screwed? Rigid or otherwise."

"You have no choice in the matter." Naked, he lifted the quilt, and got into bed. "Three months without this," he said, lying on top of John, exploring with every part of his body. "Christ! I don't know how I've survived!"

"Don't tell me you've been celibate for three months."

"Of course not. But I've been starved of you."

"What's so special about me?"

"Your arsehole. It's my property."

"Oh, no, it's not!"

"Have you slept with anyone else?" Luke asked.

"Is this important?"

"No. I'm just curious."

"I was cold," John said, laughing. "I was. Seriously. We had snow at the end of November. Not a lot, admittedly."

"Seriously cold."

"And you?"

"I never feel the cold."

"Well? Often?"

"I'm not an inveterate cottager, but I don't know what else you do in Minehead. I suppose I could have had some girls."

"Or contracted Portnoy's complaint."

"Well, that too. It's not a good substitute; you do learn something as you get older."

John shifted from under Luke's crushing weight, and said, "All that business with uncooked liver!"

"I wouldn't fancy eating it afterwards." Luke twisted John's head so that they could look at each other straight in the eye.

"Does it make any difference? That we've been promiscuous and unfaithful?"

"No."

"I'm not going back to work after Christmas. There may well be no job to go back to."

"Why, what's happened?"

"I resigned. I want to live with you more than work there."

John smiled. "I never even dared to dream . . . I was so sure you'd never say that!" Oh, but I did dream it, he said to himself. Every day you've been gone. I've handled this properly, for the first time in my life! Happiness bubbled inside him.

"The editor said I was a fool, in which opinion I'll assume he's right. I love that job. But I'd rather be with you, even if it means dole money for the duration."

"I'll rent out the pottery. And come to live with you in Somerset."

"Wait! He said I could have the holiday to think it over. But I must give him the final word on the second of January. Do you . . . do you really mean what you've just said?"

"Yes."

"Oh, Christ! John!"

John freed himself from Luke's kisses, and said, "You'll not resign. Not for me. Luke . . . " But Luke could not answer, his mouth preoccupied elsewhere. "Not that. Not tonight." He gasped as Luke twisted his nipples roughly; "Yes," he murmured. "Yes!"

"Stand up. Against the wall."

John obeyed : Luke poured oil on his shoulders, rubbed it into his back, his arms. Then pushed in his cock, very urgently. Again, John gasped. The speed of it amazed them. "Now you have it!" Luke shouted as he came, and John's hit the wall : then subsiding, subsiding, several brief starts of pleasure as they stood there, panting, exhausted, covered with sweat. Stillness. Silence. A car passed in the street below. "That was something," John whispered.

"I love you."

"I love you too. Don't go! Stay in there. Stay there all day. All night."

Luke sagged down onto the bed, pulling John with him, still inside. "I don't want to hurt you," he said. "But I do want to hurt you. Just thinking about causing pain in sex gives me an erection."

"What do you do to me? In these fantasies?"

"Tie you up to the bed. Beat you with a leather strap till you cry out for me to stop. Then cover you with kisses, in order to say I can't bear seeing you hurt . . . "

"And then?"

"Cover you from head to foot in oil and . . . fuck you till my balls are dry."

"I want that. I've always wanted that with you."

"I don't understand. Your pleasure, I mean."

"It's a kind of ultimate giving. If I can experience pain from my lover, it's . . . it's giving him everything. Everything!"

"I'm hard again already."

"I can feel it."

"I'm going to fuck you. Coming in my own come . . . " This time, Luke's teeth, biting skin on John's shoulders, drew blood. "I love you so much! I can't control it; I've never come so quickly so soon after; I can't stop . . . "

Later, they went out and bought food and wine for the week then shut themselves indoors, except for an evening at a disco, and, inevitably, a concert : seasonal pieces – carols, the *Christmas Concerto*, excerpts from *Messiah* – in the church of St Clement Danes in the Strand. The weather was raw and foggy; "Just like Dickens," Luke said with satisfaction, enjoying his survey of it from the warmth inside the flat, and most days their only taste of fresh air was when they picked up the milk from the doorstep.

Three months of separation to talk over, think about, assimilate : it all proved relatively easy. On the surface, that is. John, despite what he had said, did not delude himself that their shared life would last for ever. To move to Somerset was the best possible course of action now while existence with Luke was at its best: while the sex and the companionship worked. A cottage in the country was an investment, and letting the pottery meant he would have a base to which he could return when it all ended. A long spell

75

in Somerset might also do something for him creatively : he could, perhaps, find a studio there to rent, and the new surroundings, the new way of life, would be reflected in the pots he made.

But he was sometimes almost appalled when he considered Luke's immaturity. Luke threw himself with a puppy's enthusiasm into everything – work, the relationship, making love, even food and drink – but he rarely gave a moment's thought to what he was doing. He was totally selfish. New experience was everything, regardless of consequence or the feelings of other people. He was incapable of saying to himself : I want to do this, but I won't because it will hurt someone. Other people's emotions or points of view simply did not enter into his calculations. Calculations : quite the wrong word. Luke was the least calculating person John had ever known; he was nothing but impulses. He would not, for example, think about his sexuality : was his liking for a man something temporary; was it deep-seated? Was it connected with a refusal to accept responsibilities? He undoubtedly felt that marriage, or living with a woman, entailed more responsibilities than sharing John's bed. Was it just excitingly different, giving him the enjoyable sensation of flouting convention, bourgeois expectations? He evaded these questions when John probed, saying, "I love you. Isn't that enough?"

He says "I love you" too easily, John thought; and too often uses the word love to describe what is only a pleasurable reaction. I love Elgar (or muesli or the Princess of Wales or high-speed trains). Luke's homosexuality, he concluded, was an enjoyable holiday : adulthood would only come to him when he loved a woman. That, of course, could be years ahead. Meanwhile, he, John, might as well make the best of what he was offered, and, indeed, he did not spend all his time making a cold, careful analysis of Luke's shortcomings: it was impossible not to enjoy and marvel at the pleasure Luke gave him. There is an infectious, daft enchantment about this man, he said to himself : I do love him very much.

But there was one terrible fear he did not like to contemplate, worse than the mental and emotional condition he might be in when their affair was over (that period, however painful, would surely be temporary) : Luke would destroy his creativity. Since they had met, John's skill and inventiveness with clay had grown beyond anything he had previously thought possible. Luke gave him space and time and ability to dig inside himself and bring out, in his work, an artistry he had never realised was there. His lover, going, might kill it, maybe on purpose; or even before he went he would damage it irretrievably.

They went to search for clothes, in Selfridges of all places. Luke bought a suit for the wedding; he had not owned a suit, he said, since he was a kid. It made him look elegant, John said. And sexy. Sexy? Yes. Tight trousers; they showed his legs off beautifully, his supple thighs, thick and muscular. And a very interesting bulge. The assistant, overhearing their conversation, looked embarrassed, and most disapproving when Luke decided to walk out of the shop wearing his purchase. At the top of the escalator they met Kevin, who was escaping early from the boredom of Christmas in Gloucester and buying wine glasses, Cheryl and Aaron's wedding present.

"What *are* you doing dressed up like that?" he asked.

"Going down," said Luke. "John, this is Kevin. Kevin . . . are you busy?"

"No."

"Good. You're coming out with us for a celebration lunch."

"What are we supposed to be celebrating?"

"The fact that John is going to live with me in Somerset. Oh, it's ages since I saw you!" And as they stepped off the escalator Luke kissed him.

Luke and John drove down to Okehampton the day before the wedding, Kevin with them; all three were to stay overnight at Cheryl's parents. In the car, on the way down, Kevin was making the Sullivan family Christmas in Gloucester sound like exile on a desert island. "There must be a few big butch men," Luke said. "Make your eyes water, like I would."

"Did he ever tell you, John, he once spent the night with me?" Kevin tickled the back of Luke's neck.

"Don't interfere with the driver," Luke said.

"He came staggering into our flat, gone midnight and dead drunk. Jack was away. He passed out unconscious on the sofa, so I undressed him and lugged him into bed."

"I don't remember a thing about it, but it must have been the most exciting moment of your life, Kevin. Me! Stark naked and defenceless."

"It was in your heterosexual days, and you were *stinking* of booze."

"I woke up in the morning not knowing where I was, lying next to somebody I imagined was female. Then I saw it was him!"

"Nothing nicer in your lover's absence than having a drunken het in your bed, snoring all night. Ugh!"

Towards Bristol the weather grew worse. It had stayed cold all Christmas week, with frost and a few flurries of snow, the temperature hardly rising above freezing point. Now there was fog again. At first it only slowed the car down to forty, but as they drove on into Somerset it became dense and froze on the windscreen. Luke tried to follow the red lights in front, but when the car left the motorway there was nothing. Twenty miles an hour was now too fast. The journey, which had been easy, was suddenly nerve-racking; the light-hearted fun of the conversation died altogether as the three of them peered into the gloom, trying to find anything, a car, a tree, an exit sign, that would give them some sort of confidence, some assurance that they would not crash to a certain death. Luke pulled out into the middle, afraid that in the slow lane he might run into the back of a vehicle travelling at even more of a snail's pace than he was, and seconds later he found he was passing a lorry; its tail-lights were not working. No one commented. Perhaps the others had not realised how near they were to a collision, which, if not fatal, would undoubtedly have ruined the whole trip. Luke breathed heavily, and told himself to keep calm.

"Shall I drive?" John asked. "It is my car, after all."

"We'll stop at the next service station."

The heater stopped working; the fog, presumably, was the cause, but John couldn't understand why. Eventually frost began to form on the inside of the windows; Kevin, in the back, and wrapped up in the quilt he had brought, watched his breath form white fern patterns on the glass. An hour later, tense and with a headache beginning to throb, Luke saw the sign for Taunton Deane services.

"That's Jack's Audi!" Kevin exclaimed. His stomach lurched uncomfortably and his heart raced: he had not anticipated meeting so soon; he had rehearsed, many times, what they would say when they met in the lounge of the farm, had prepared himself for a variety of different receptions. But coming across Jack so unexpectedly seemed to destroy what little confidence he had. He thought for one wild moment of staying in the car while the others went into the cafeteria, but that was impossible. He got out, and stood in the freezing swirling fog, bewildered and frightened.

Jack was sitting facing away from them. Luke crept up behind. "Guess who," he said, and put his hands over Jack's eyes.

"Luke!" Jack heaved a great sigh of relief. "And John! I kept hoping all the way down I'd meet you somewhere! I've come from Liverpool. Hullo, Kevin."

"Hullo."

They looked at each other, their expressions giving nothing away. There was a short embarrassed silence, then Luke said, "We've news for you. We're leaving London for good."

"You . . . and John?"

"Well it isn't me and Kevin. Do you want a coffee?"

"Please. Where are you going to live?"

"Somewhere near Minehead."

"Oh. What did you buy them for a wedding present? I seem to have spent a fortune in Heals."

"One of the many things gay people miss out on," Kevin said. "When we decide it's for life, no one coughs up with wedding presents. When I moved in with Jack I didn't even own my own towel."

"And those two don't need anything. What do you get for a man who can buy a house by writing a cheque on his own bank account?"

No one could think of a reply to that.

"I'll get the coffees," Kevin said, glad to escape. When he returned Jack was saying how frightening it was driving alone in the fog. He'd had this awful sensation of unreality, of feeling he was in a dream and that any crazy thing he might do would only have one consequence, that he would wake up in bed in the flat in Greenwich. "I'll come with you," Kevin said. "If . . . you'd like."

"Yes. I would." Jack smiled at him. Kevin's heart leaped: perhaps it was going to be all right. Dear God, please, it was going to be all right!

When they resumed the journey, John took over. He kept his eyes firmly on the red lights of the Audi, which Kevin was now driving. "Have you always kissed your male friends when you see them in public?" he asked.

"Shocking, isn't it! Tch, tch! And in Selfridges too!"

"Well, have you?"

"Jack and Kevin, yes, sometimes. Don't ask me why, because I don't know. Next question: have I ever been to bed with either of them. Answer: no. And I don't want to either. Jack Crawley . . . he was the first gay person I met."

"When was that?"

"At school. No, we didn't even have a quick wank in the bog. I was far too interested in girls."

"I think you're rather patronising to Kevin. About being gay."

"Absolute rubbish!"

"You still feel . . . you're somehow superior."

"What on earth do you mean?"

"Teasing Kevin about big butch men. Saying you could make his eyes water. The assumption that you're a real male and he's not. The assumption that he only likes playing one role in bed. Hinting you've a great big cock and he hasn't, that all the goodies are in the size of the real man's organ."

"You're seeing far too much in it that wasn't intended!"

"It's degrading."

"To whom?"

"Both of you."

"It's a joke, that's all. Do you think he's envious, then? Wants to be a big hearty he-man?"

"There you are again! All this emphasis on big! And, no, I don't think he's envious. That's why it's so silly."

"He's perfectly happy to be Kevin? Glad to be gay, as the song has it? Well, I agree with you."

"Good."

"So what are we arguing about?"

"Conditioned reflexes you'd be nicer without."

"You do sound prim. Are we having a quarrel?"

"Yes."

He laughed. "Let's concentrate on the fog, shall we? You nearly hit the crash barrier just now. Where are we, anyway?"

"God knows. Wellington, I think."

"Do you love me?"

"And all your very evident warts. Yes."

"Anyway, I have got a big cock." He giggled. "You ought to know that. A *huge* one!"

"For Christ's sake, Luke!"

Chapter Six

People expected to suffer in the church, but the new heating system proved very efficient. Feet were cold, but no one was shivering. There she was, entering the north door; they all stood as the organ triumphantly rang out the B flat of the piece from *Lohengrin:* heads turned, though at first it was impossible to know it was her as opposed to any other bride, for the cloud of white satin and lace masked her identity. But as she slowly moved up the nave, leaning on her father's arm, she was recognizably Cheryl, even if it was a Cheryl only glimpsed infrequently: shy and pale, the usually flashing dark eyes now lacklustre, and a fixed smile that seemed to be saying she wished she was a thousand miles away.

Dearly beloved, we are gathered together here in the sight of God, and in the face of this congregation, to join together this man and this woman in holy matrimony; which is an honourable estate, instituted of God in the time of man's innocency . . .

We have no benefit of clergy; no rituals, no families who gather together to rejoice. But Kevin and I were once an honourable estate. Nothing can alter the truth of that.

My parents were married in this church a quarter of a century ago. Standing on that same spot.

. . . therefore is not by any to be enterprised, nor taken in hand unadvisedly, lightly, or wantonly, to satisfy men's carnal lusts and appetites, like brute beasts that have no understanding; but reverently, discreetly, advisedly, soberly, and in the fear of God . . .

Are women not thought capable of experiencing carnal lusts and appetites? John glanced at Luke. A brute beast *with* understanding? Reverent, discreet, advised? Huh! With my body I him worship. The legs in the new suit trousers.

. . . it was ordained for the mutual society, help, and comfort that the one ought to have of the other, both in prosperity and adversity.

We have that without the necessity of sacrament. Kevin!

. . . if either of you know any impediment, why ye may not be joined together in matrimony, ye do now confess it. For be ye well assured, that so many as are coupled together otherwise than God's word doth allow are not joined together by God; neither is their matrimony lawful.

She had been shaken by meeting John, much more than she thought she would be. What an ugly, unattractive, sexless man! Whatever did Luke find in him? Luke had, it is true, been little in her thoughts since she had met him on the bus that Saturday morning, but seeing them together, yesterday, had upset her to a surprising degree. Luke was out of reach for ever. In the pause that followed the clergyman's words, she hoped, for one absurd moment, that he would shout "Stop!" or "I object!" and rush forward, grab her arm and run out of the church with her. There was a long silence. She wanted to turn her head and look at him. So. It was the god-like Aaron, and indeed he was like a god or the statue of one, particularly now in a dazzling white suit that eclipsed even her yards of white satin. A brief moment of sun, a shaft of light through a window, made radiant the pale blond waves of his hair. He lacked only the guitar and a microphone to make the congregation worship. But antiseptic, not Luke with his all-too-human blemishes of white skin and spots and armpit smells, his chest too hairy like a hearthrug (hearthrugs have dog smells, human smells): alive with the quarrels and violence and selfishness inflicted, the profundity of emotion he had once felt for her and stirred in her.

"I will," said Aaron, almost unable to speak. His tongue was leaden, his mouth aching as if lockjaw gripped it. There were tears in his eyes. The beauty of the words, the power of ceremony to transcend everything: he was astonished at what he was finding inside himself. He had never in his whole life been moved in this way, had considered it only softness in soppy wet people.

. . . wilt thou love (she had insisted that "obey" and "serve" should be deleted), honour, and keep him in sickness and in health; and, forsaking all other, keep thee only unto him, so long as ye both shall live?

"I will." Clear and unflustered her voice. She should be saying that to me. What have I done? Cheryl and I on that spot, there, where Mum and Dad stood. Christ, what have I done? Luke felt himself blush as the emotion surged up in him. Dad's face, only hours before he died: "She's got class," he'd said, unreservedly approving his younger son's choice. Why did you have to die, you inconsiderate old *sod*? Help me! I *need* you! No, no. He made himself calm a little, then turned and smiled at John.

With this ring I thee wed, with my body I thee worship, and with all my worldly goods I thee endow . . .

Worldly goods? Yes. He glanced at his own ring, the bloodstone Jack had given him. Whatever happens to us, I'll never give it back, never not wear it: he's too much part of me.

Those whom God hath joined together let no man put asunder.

It will not be me.

It could be me. Hell, what nonsense! Just the emotion of the occasion. This was why Luke hated ritual so much; it took away the processes of rational thinking, gave bogus sanctification to what were no more than hopes, aspirations and beginnings that might collapse soon enough; it extracted promises no one knew if they'd be able to keep, chained two people together under the insidious spell of some spurious religiosity that was supposed to . . . what? The sentence, toppling over, made him lose his train of thought.

I pronounce that they be man and wife together, in the name of the Father and of the Son, and of the Holy Ghost.

It's done. No going back.

I should see my parents now I'm here. But Kevin and I must talk. I won't go alone; four years I've said I won't return unless he's with me. Crawl back without him? Told you so! We were right! Perhaps you see the error of your ways. No!

Now for the jollifications. Photographs (not a great many, please; it's too cold). Food and wine. All these super hats. It's snowing outside! Why's Luke so serious, his face all thunder?

Mr and Mrs Aaron Brown. That Brown, awful, ugly name. She looks gorgeous, that tight dress round her breasts, her hips. In sickness and in health. His right leg still dragged.

You can't alter what has been, for two years the shared home, shared bed, lives inextricably one. All that I've left inside her mind, her heart, physically left inside her body: no trace, no mark, nothing? I can't believe it!

It was snowing heavily, and the wind, quite strong now, whipped it into their faces, already was drifting it against gravestones and buttresses. Photography was abandoned; neither Cheryl nor Aaron minded, but Doris was upset. She'd looked forward to a print of them standing at the porch; she'd frame it and place it beside the one in the lounge of Peter and Susan. That fine autumn day outside the island's ancient parish church: far too young they were, just kids! David and Pat on a baking hot August Saturday, some awful Methodist church in Colchester, had been lost in the flood. Martin and Ann were not photographed: so soon after the flood their wedding and her camera missing, washed out to sea most like. Such a pity.

A fleet of cars took them to the farm. Cheryl had persuaded her parents not to hold the reception at a hotel; there would be thirty-nine guests in all and the house was big enough, just the right size in fact. A hotel, a sit-down meal; it was so impersonal, and besides, the farm was isolated, well away from any attentions the press might give them. Aaron was, after all, supposed to be famous; a crowd of unwanted people from the music world might ruin everything. As it turned out not one reporter or photographer came. She wondered why: had they been one hundred per cent successful in keeping their plans secret? Or was it the weather? Or was Aaron not worth any interest now? No downfall was so rapid as that of a pop star out of fashion. A year ago it would have been different: screaming girls, tv cameras. Misery! Aaron's Rod had disbanded but they were all here today, and were going to perform later, a final farewell.

At the top of the stairs she met Luke. "May I kiss the bride?" he asked.

"Yes."

A gentle peck. He looked round; no one, so he pulled her close and kissed her, a kiss like it once was. She freed herself. "What have we done!" he said.

"Don't be ridiculous."

"Cheryl!"

"Stop acting as if you were someone out of a romantic novel! You never did know how to behave."

"I'm sorry." He stood aside and let her through. She hesitated for a fraction of a second.

"It's too late."

"If you ever want me . . ."

She went into her room and slammed the door. Once hers, then shared with Luke, now where she'd sleep tonight with Ron. There was to be no honeymoon; in the circumstances it seemed pointless, and anyway, they'd only recently returned from Spain. Last night Aaron had stayed at the White Hart in Okehampton, a gesture to propriety they'd both thought ridiculous, but necessary. Having lived together, to be married under the old dispensation had not proved totally easy; the customs involved did not sit on them joyously. Hours later, excited and happy with food, wine, friends, dancing, she suddenly remembered this scene with Luke and laughed to herself, dismissed it for the silly nonsense it obviously was. Cheryl Brown, not Demelza Poldark.

"Your Aunt Dorothy is looking embarrassed," Aaron said. "Why are you laughing at her?"

It was a good wedding Luke thought, the reception magnificent, the setting perfect: the old farmhouse with its low beamed ceilings and huge rooms and roaring fires, the wind howling outside and snow fluttering in the afternoon dusk, Dartmoor huge and inhospitable under a thin dusting of white. The snow was not bad enough to make guests leave early, fearful of drifts and being unable to reach home, but it was just sufficient to emphasise the warmth and pleasure indoors and the cold, almost bluish, beauty outside. People could feel pleasurably cut off from the rest of humanity, a satisfying sensation when they, not the weather, still held control of the roads. Luke poured himself more champagne, glad that his capacity for this drink was endless. He rejoined John and Kevin, who were both on top form: the wine had done its work with them but not yet wreaked havoc, or maybe their happiness was for other reasons; John, that separation was ended, and Kevin, Luke imagined (he did not know, but the signs were there), with Jack, as he damned well ought to be, silly boy.

Kevin tugged his sleeve. "Do you know there are two other gay people here?"

"Who?" Luke asked.

"The best man, no less."

"What, the Spaniard?"

"Ramón, yes. And that other friend of Ron's, the tall thin

professor-like one, Tim something."

"How do you know?"

Kevin laughed. "One can tell."

"How?"

"Eye contact."

"Ah, you're inventing. Gay people always fantasise that half the world is like themselves. Aaron's two closest friends! Not very likely."

"Superior again," John muttered. "Sometimes I'm ashamed to be with you. 'Gay people always fantasise' etcetera. What the hell do you know about it?" He turned to Kevin. "Are they an affair?" he asked.

"I haven't found out. Yet. I'll send you a report." Kevin slipped away, but not to spy on the two suspected persons. He was with Jack, the two of them in a corner, apart from everyone else.

A good wedding, Luke thought again, as he swallowed the champagne in one mouthful. Plenty of drink and all his favourite food: quiches, pizzas, things on sticks, anchovies, asparagus, pineapple, trifles, treacle flans, cherry ginger crunch, syllabub! And the cheeses! A really soft crumbling Stilton, Brie so runny it looked like squashed fruit! "Will you propose my mother-in-law's health?" Aaron asked. "Mother-in-law? Oh, yes . . . yes, of course. My surrogate mother." He did so, referring to the Woods as his adopted parents, "though we've never made it legal," he said. Later, he said to Cheryl's father that he often wished they had made it legal. He couldn't be closer in their affections than he was already, Mr Wood answered, and added, almost as an afterthought, that he didn't want any more of the car money.

"Car money?"

"The loan," Mr Wood said. "The money you borrowed. In other words –" for Luke still looked puzzled – "you don't have to pay it back."

"I couldn't agree to that!" Luke was shocked, and humbled. "Oh, you old fool, you're going to make me cry." He averted his face. "I don't deserve anything from you, from you least of all!"

"Luke." Cheryl's mother took both his hands. "You must stop thinking that. She's married now. You've both done what you want and you're both happy, I'm sure. Just come and see us more often. There's nothing left you have to regret, daft child, or for us to forgive."

He clasped her tight, buried his face in her hair. Now they were both crying.

"The agony!" Aaron mocked. "Oh, the pain! The tears!"

She pulled herself free, laughing, and said, "Two sons!"

"This is far too emotional," Luke objected. "Quite ridiculous!"

John joined the group. "Whatever's going on?" he asked. Luke explained, then turned to thank Cheryl's parents again, but the moment of melodrama had passed and they'd moved away, Mrs Wood to speak to her sister, and Mr Wood to check that there was no shortage of drink.

For it was New Year's Eve. The intention was that the party would continue until the small hours, so, with the exception of a few people who had to go elsewhere to celebrate, they would all see the New Year in together, bride and groom included. Where everyone would sleep was not quite clear; it was Mrs Wood's biggest headache. Luke and his friend could have the single beds in the spare room; and Mary, the bridesmaid, could have a bed made up on the landing where Jack had dossed down last night, but Ray, and was it Tim, would have to have armchairs. She could put a camp bed in the kitchen for Cheryl's old school-friend, Linda. (Her family had moved to Wales, though perhaps the other two girls, Louise and Paula, who still lived in town, might take her home with them). Fortunately the Brown contingent were booked into the White Hart, and all the other relatives lived locally, but what about Jack and Kevin? Kevin had spent last night on the sofa. Jack could have the floor; no, she couldn't let him sleep on the floor. Well, maybe there were enough cushions . . .

"Why were you looking so serious in church?" John asked.

"A bad dream," Luke said.

"I thought so."

"Meaning?"

"Actually seeing Cheryl married."

"I did . . . I admit . . . feel jealous. I nearly shouted 'I forbid the banns', like something out of Jane Eyre. Very stupid."

"No."

"It passed as quickly as it came. Bloody religious ceremonies, twisting and warping everything!"

"I'm glad it passed as quickly as it came." Just a touch of malice. They smiled at each other.

"Look, love . . . where are we going to live? We haven't even

87

discussed it properly! And I have to go back to work the day after tomorrow."

"As you said, I can stay at your digs for a bit. While we go on a cottage hunt. No, not that sort of cottage! If I can get a mortgage, I can put down the deposit. I've saved enough."

"I really ought to be paying half."

"You can pay me some rent."

"Rent boy Luke, is it?"

"Arseholes!"

"Precisely. It doesn't seem right, somehow." Luke shook his head.

"When you want to leave me, as you inevitably will do, you'll be free. No unpleasant legal tangles to sort out."

Luke stared at him. "I sometimes think you're the one who likes to cause the pain," he said.

"I'm only being realistic."

"You do know how to kick in the balls. So bloody well!"

"Maybe that's love."

"Buy your shitty cottage, then. But I'll show you who's S and who's M! I've a good mind to rape you on this carpet."

"In front of all these people?"

"Shut up and kiss me."

"Don't be so silly!"

The dancing had started. Aaron, no longer in his white suit, was dressed in a more familiar skin of jeans and tee-shirt. He was singing all the numbers the group had made popular, making no concession to the fact that this audience was not a crowd of adulatory teenagers. Its older members might have heard him on the albums their children possessed or even seen him on *Top of the Pops,* a programme they would doubtless not have watched from choice, but their young might have slaughtered them if they had switched it off. Yet no one stood listening, or passing critical comments; everybody danced: even Kevin, who loathed dancing with women, was cavorting with Cheryl's Aunt Dorothy.

"Increasingly not our scene," he said to Jack, when they were alone.

"Yes. Let's go."

"Can we?"

Jack looked at his watch. "What would you say to leaving at about ten and going to Torquay? See the New Year in at the club."

Kevin's eyes lit up. "I'd say yes!!"

"Good. We'll do that then."

"But . . . are we coming back here?"

"No." There had been no chance to talk yesterday except in the car, and the problem of fog had forced out other considerations. So, little was said. Perhaps it was not necessary: they both knew, without discussing it, that the long separation was over. It had seemed very hard, therefore, being under the same roof but apart, and Jack, too tensed up to sleep, had thought it unkind of the Woods to treat him and Kevin differently from the other couples. Accepting us socially, yes, but sharing one of the beds! A different matter! Or did it just simply not occur to either of them? A nice irony was that Luke and John had shared a bedroom: because Cheryl's parents don't know about that particular set-up, he guessed, rightly.

Kevin looked thoughtful. "Where *are* we going to stay tonight?"

"Secret. Tell you later."

"A mystery tour! I'd like that."

"Look at Cheryl!"

She was watching Aaron. Yes, she was thinking, he *can* still do it; the spell is still there! But it was an effort: the sexy teenager was an act; he'd moved on, grown up. That moustache! It looked so silly! What would there be now that he would become much more of a private person? That little episode with Luke was nothing, of no significance. She could find everything she wanted with Ron. She had to now.

The group played for five minutes without him while he went in search of a beer. He passed Jack and Kevin who were standing next to Tim and Ray; "You four should get to know each other," he said, as he poured out a drink. "You've all got something in common."

They looked at each other, then Ray said, "We'd guessed."

"And I knew," Jack replied.

"Four," said Kevin. "Five with John. Do we count Luke? Yes, of course. Five and three-quarters. And there's thirty-nine people here. Somewhat higher than the average statistics lay down for our guidance."

"As the great man said. Maybe it tells us something about our straight friends."

"Maybe it's an accident," Jack suggested.

"Are you . . . lovers?" Kevin asked.

"No," Tim said. "We were. Sort of. A long time ago."

"We're going in a minute, to the club in Torquay. Do you want to come with us?"

"Why not. Ray?"

"Yes. It's very nice, this," – Ray gestured round the room – "but it always hits home when the dancing begins. Oh so long as we act like everyone else, i.e. pretend we're just like them. If we started doing what's natural to us, i.e. dancing with each other, they'd all have hysterics. Except Ron and Cheryl, of course."

"Ray's a great campaigner," Tim explained. "CHE marches. That's why he talks in i.e.'s. Though he's right, of course. Luke . . . Luke . . . has nice eyes."

Kevin laughed. "Not a chance, mate."

It was two in the morning before Cheryl and Aaron got to bed. They were both exhausted. She had no romantic illusions about her wedding day being the most important of her life, and indeed it had begun badly with her nervousness at church, her feelings about Luke (a result of panic, she decided, when faced with the truth that she no longer had the power to choose); but the afternoon and evening were memorable, would stay with her, pleasurably, as long as she lived: never again would so many close friends and members of her family come together to share her happiness and wish her well.

"I was on form," Aaron said, as he undressed. "What did you think?"

"You were."

"I've been wondering."

"What about?"

"The future. Becoming a flamenco expert, taking classical music lessons. I can't do it. Ray told me that, years ago." She stared at him. "I'd never succeed. I ought to stick to what I can do."

"Oh, no!"

"I don't mean Aaron's Rod. That's dead, gone for ever. I mean . . . re-model my career as a rock singer. I don't know how. Yet." She said nothing. "You don't approve?"

"It's not that."

"You feel I'd have another attack, I'd become really ill. I don't think so." He climbed into bed beside her. "I'm still good, aren't I?

Well . . . aren't I?"

"Yes."

"You're not sure."

"Yes, I'm sure."

"Look . . . I know it's our wedding night and all that. But I'm knackered."

She was relieved. "So am I."

"Shall we just go to sleep then?"

"Yes."

He turned over, away from her. It was a long time, however, before she slept. Too much excitement, she thought, too much wine. She could hear Luke and John laughing helplessly in the next room. Jack and Kevin, perhaps, were still raving it up at Torquay. She suddenly felt depressed, as if the fun had been extinguished for ever.

"Jack, I don't know whether I want to go through with this."

"Please."

"We could go to the farm. The back door will be open, they said."

"Kevin . . . !"

He sighed. "All right."

Jack unlocked the door of his parents' house: he had never returned his key. All was quiet. There had evidently been a party, glasses and empty bottles in the lounge, plates stacked but unwashed in the kitchen. They took off their shoes and crept upstairs to Jack's room, feeling like conspirators. Kevin wanted to giggle, but wisely checked the impulse. The room, Jack could see at a glance, had not been used for a long time; his bed was in its usual place but without any sheets or blankets, and the furniture, not arranged in any particular order or pattern, looked as if it was only being stored there. It was bitterly cold, but fortunately they had with them the quilt Kevin had brought from the flat.

"I was beginning to forget how beautiful you are," Jack whispered, exploring.

"*Now?* Three o'clock in the morning?"

"Yes. Oh yes! After all this time."

"I love you. I'll never leave you again."

"Don't. It doesn't matter."

"Can you forget it?"

"It doesn't matter. You're here now and I love you."

"I'm not worth it."

"Shut up."

"My love!"

In the morning Jack was up almost as soon as he woke. He had not drawn the curtains when they went to bed, hoping that the daylight would disturb him early. The windows were all steamed over; he rubbed them and looked out at the familiar houses of his childhood. The Skinners had cut down the fir tree in their front garden: yesterday's snow was still there, and a thick frost; the wind was bitter and the sky full of heavy dark cloud.

Kevin slept on. Jack kissed him; the face was serene and happy. They were about to start all over again: he was as excited, as quivering and joyous as when he had begun to understand, at the end of their first term at the university, some of the potential there could be in his relationship with this beautiful and fascinating boy. I could spend my life in his company, he had thought, and not grow tired of him.

But now, at this moment, there could well be trouble. Noises came from his parents' bedroom: his mother. He waited until she had gone downstairs to the kitchen, then followed her.

"Jack!!" She ran forward and threw her arms round him. "Why? How . . . ?"

"I thought you'd like me to wish you a happy New Year," he said, grinning.

"Oh . . .! Wait a minute. I think I'm going to cry."

"Mother!"

She sniffed, but steadied herself. "It's such a shock. And . . . so early in the morning! How . . . where did you stay last night?"

"Here. We let ourselves in with my key."

"We?"

"Kevin's here."

"Oh." The pleasure vanished from her face. There was a sickening lurch in his stomach. "Where did you sleep?"

He lit a cigarette, his hands shaking. "Mother, you must accept it."

"I think you'd better tell your father when he gets up that one of you spent the night on the sofa." She filled the kettle and lit the gas. "Would you like a cup of tea?" She stared at him. "I . . . can't accept it. I've tried. I've tried. And I can't." He said nothing. "We

92

always liked him, were quite happy when we thought you were just friends. But when you told us that . . . the pair of you doing that . . ."

"I said nothing about what we might or might not do."

She shuddered. "Where was the fault? That's what I keep wondering. What caused it? Was it us?"

She was older than he remembered, more lined, greyer. Less energy. Unmistakeably middle-aged, of another era, of another set of values than he was. "There is no fault," he said, gently. "It just is. I'm happy. That's all that matters."

"Dad won't be up for hours," she said, changing the subject. "He had quite a few drinks last night." She managed a smile. "Thank goodness he doesn't have to open the bank on New Year's Day!"

"Shall I . . . wake Kevin, before . . ."

"Yes. Then you could say you just happened to be passing. It . . . would be tactful."

He frowned. "All right."

"So, what are you doing here? You didn't really come all this way just to wish us the compliments of the season. I'm not that daft!"

"We came down for a wedding. Cheryl Wood. Do you remember her?"

"Cheryl! Why, I was talking to her aunt, Dorothy Ash; you know her. It was only last week! She never said anything about it."

"It was kept very quiet. She was marrying somebody famous. Who was famous."

"Really! Who?"

"A pop star. Aaron of Aaron's Rod."

"No, dear, I don't think I've heard of him. We don't listen to that sort of thing very much. Cheryl Wood married! I'm glad it wasn't Luke Edwards. She was well rid of him! Behaving like that after her parents had taken him in and treated him like a son. Dreadful!"

"I'll go and wake Kevin."

It was an uneasy couple of hours and they were glad to leave. Kevin hated every second of it; why on earth did he bother, he asked Jack when they were driving up to the moor afterwards. Because, Jack answered, the door was ajar now. He felt quite pleased in fact; it could have been a lot worse. There had been no arguments. And no prohibitions – stated, that is – on their coming again; his mother seemed sad, at the moment of parting, that he was not staying longer. The conversation, however, had been difficult, particularly when his father appeared, but at least it was polite. Kevin, unsure of what to say or to do, had remained almost totally silent. Jack kept wishing that Owen was there to help. His brother would have said exactly what he felt about it all. But Owen was in Edinburgh, though he had been down for Christmas, Mrs Crawley told him, puffing fat cigars and driving a brand new sports car. He had plenty of girl-friends these days, she said when Jack asked if he was still going around with Lesley, but no one serious. Love 'em and leave 'em, that was Owen: time yet for him to settle when he'd found the right one. And I've found the right one, Jack thought; why can't they see that? Is gender the sole question of importance?

Mr Crawley stayed only half an hour before announcing that he had a lot of work to do in the garden. A record number of Christmas cards they'd had this year, he told Jack, more than a hundred. The Wilsons held their usual party on Boxing Day, same old crowd there. He'd changed the car a few months ago. The traffic jams in town were horrendous last summer; all that the M5 had done was to shift the bottleneck from Exeter to their very own doorstep. And the government were still dithering over the various routes for the new bypass. The north side of town made more sense in his opinion . . . He went out and began digging in the vegetable patch. He wouldn't if we weren't here, Jack thought: it's freezing cold and the ground's so hard with frost that it's pointless. His father, he was surprised to notice, had not aged at all. The same fierce eyes and moustache, the same negative kind of energy.

Mrs Crawley fussed round, cooking them a large breakfast, keeping the conversation to platitudes and gossip about friends and neighbours. She addressed nearly all her remarks to her son, but whether she was ignoring Kevin deliberately, or from a kind of nervousness, Jack wasn't sure. However, she did offer Kevin another cup of tea and told him to help himself to more toast; then asked, though she did not pay much attention to his answer, if he liked the school where he was teaching. "Keep in touch," she said to Jack, when they were, for a moment, alone. "Ring me. You haven't forgotten the number?"

"No."

"I miss you terribly." She stared out of the window. Jack gripped her arm.

Tim and Ray were not at the farmhouse. Ray had phoned: things had got complicated last night; he was at Paignton, and Tim had ended up somewhere near Totnes. No, they wouldn't be back till evening. Totnes! Tim, Jack remembered, had spent much of the night in Hugh's company; they had probably gone to the restaurant. He remembered Ray talking to a slim fair-haired boy, but he hadn't taken much notice: dancing as he was with Kevin for the first time in months, there was no desire at all to keep abreast of the usual intrigue of the club.

They decided to go over to the estuary, the six of them, for a pub lunch, a walk, then tea at the cottage. The sun came out just before they arrived, shafts of dazzling light from behind dark clouds, glittering coldly on the sea. The mud, Cheryl thought, was like grey paint: miles of it, enough for all the world's battleships. The birds, as always, stood on the wet pewter surface in their hundreds, deep in contemplation.

"Wallow in glorious mud," said Aaron. They were on top of the wall, heading for the Turf. On the land side the ground was hard, the fields prickly with frost. Half a dozen bedraggled cows stared, or tried to feed on the unappetising grass. "I have this insane desire sometimes to throw off all my clothes and writhe around in it."

"Insane is right," Cheryl said. "Do you want to freeze to death?"

"I don't mean now."

"I like it," said Luke. "The idea appeals."

"I could sell you then," John said, "as a sculpture in clay. Might make my fortune."

"I once saw a film which had a scene with all these women fighting in a mud-bath. Very sexy. Can't remember anything else about it."

"A wrestling-match in the mud." Aaron looked at him. "Why not?"

"You're on," Luke answered. "But we'll leave it till the weather's warmer."

"Stupid male chauvinists trying to prove their virility," Kevin said. "That's all it is."

"Is it?" John asked. "Maybe they fancy each other." The subject changed; why, Aaron wanted to know, were homosexuals so promiscuous? They only had to go out for an evening (he was

95

obviously thinking of Ray and Tim) and it was simply a case of finding a body for the night. Cattle-market stuff. Straight people were just the same, Jack said, and where was Ron's evidence? He hadn't himself read any information on the subject. And if gay love-affairs didn't last as long as some heterosexual marriages, it was more to do with society's pressures than promiscuity.

"Everyone wants a stable loving relationship," Kevin said. "Yet there's this urge to know what the other girl or the other man is like. I thought the two were compatible, but I don't any longer."

"Till the next time," Luke teased.

"And only if you cheat and lie and time-table things with such clockwork precision that the fun is spoiled," Jack said.

"What do you know about it?" Cheryl asked Aaron.

"I've had my moments," he answered.

"I fail to understand the need." She was puzzled. "I don't understand it at all. Why shouldn't one man be enough, be absolute?"

"One man doesn't necessarily satisfy everything," Kevin said.

"When we're with you lot," Aaron said, "we always end up talking about gay life and nothing else."

"Not true."

"Oh, but it is!" Jack sided with Ron. "We bore other people, sympathetic people like you, bore them rigid! We're obsessive!"

"I'm not bored," Cheryl said.

"I am," said Aaron.

They were approaching the lock-gates. The Turf looked deserted and peaceful in the winter light. A cat dozed on the path, and an ancient dappled horse champed the grass in the garden.

The pub was empty, so they crowded round the fire, eating ploughmans and drinking bitter. Luke was in philosophical mood. What had his generation achieved; what was it likely to achieve? They had no good examples from the people ahead of them, the men and women in their thirties and forties. Where were the promising young musicians, the budding poets and painters? There was no Keats, no Mozart, no Picasso: no Wilfred Owen and Siegfried Sassoon, scarcely older than he was, poring for hours over different drafts of *Dulce et Decorum est*. No composer of any significance had been born since Benjamin Britten, and that was nearly seventy years ago. People only seemed interested in personal relationships and the trivia of who was sleeping with who.

96

"We're free to do as we please, more than anyone has ever been," Kevin said. "Perhaps we've opted for seeking fulfilment in other ways."

"Balls," Luke answered. "All balls. You can still have a happy love-life or sex-life and create great art."

"When do *you* begin?" John asked.

"It's all right for you."

"Maybe with every single craft almost dead or forgotten," Jack said, "and art so complex and private, the will to succeed like that has gone. I mean it must have been easy for the Elizabethans. Most of them could dash off a passable sonnet about their mistress's eyebrows."

"So we turn to the few simpler crafts that are left? Pottery. Sorry, my love."

"No, no," John conceded. "It's probably true."

"Or children's books. Or pop music."

"This discussion is becoming boring," said Aaron. "If it's not gay life, it's a bleeding university lecture analysing everything instead of getting on with it."

"Hear, hear," said Cheryl.

"Such loyalty!" Luke was sarcastic. "Ron, I'm jealous of you. You *have* achieved something." Though that isn't why he's jealous, John thought. "Jack and me and Kevin, we have degrees; Jack has a first, but what does it mean? We've been educated with great intensity into being spectators at the sport. I could write you a cogent analysis of the imagery in the later poetry of W.B. Yeats, but why did nobody ever consider it worthwhile trying to show me how to write a poem of my own?"

"Market forces," Aaron said. The others laughed. "No, I mean it. What would be the use of five thousand poets graduating every year? There'd be a run on the pound and five thousand more write-offs in the dole queues."

"Just as pointless as five thousand people understanding 'Byzantium' or 'Among Schoolchildren' and writing alpha plus essays on the subject."

"Not at all. With that, you can organise industry, teach, publish, go into tv or the theatre. Run the Labour Party. Even turn into a smart young journalist."

"Maybe you're right," Luke said. "But it makes me sick." He walked over to the window and stared gloomily out at the estuary.

97

"Teach, did you say?" Jack asked, laughing. "Do you know how many unemployed teachers there are? At the Social Security near my school even the people *behind* the counter are out-of-work teachers!"

"Let's go back to the cottage," Aaron said.

They retraced their steps along the wall, each couple huddling close for warmth. "There are plenty of things worth doing," Kevin said to Jack. "Trying to achieve a society where I can walk with you like I am now any time, any place. Where every gay in a tv comedy show isn't a queen waving a handbag."

"A long time in the future."

"The future!" Cheryl was listening. "I'll be pregnant."

"You'll be a great-grandmother, more like."

"If you're not pregnant it won't be for the want of trying," Aaron said.

"Perhaps I am already."

"Do you really think so?" John asked, almost anxiously.

"Little Aaronlets swimming around inside you," Luke said.

"Like sharks, I suppose. Swimming around! Your biology's defective."

"Mine wasn't this morning," Aaron said.

"You're confusing the issue. Biology's not the same as plumbing."

"Issue! That's good!"

"Note the plural," Cheryl said. "How many does he think the human female carries at one time? Maybe the boys at our school only learned about rabbits."

Jack and Kevin, ahead of the others, stopped. The wall was too narrow to let anybody pass, so they all stood, arms round each other. "Why are we waiting?" Luke sang. In his donkey jacket and bobble hat he looked like a council workman: like his father, Cheryl thought. Aaron, in a white sheepskin coat, seemed almost absurdly different.

"We're absorbing the view," Jack answered.

"There's a lot of it," Kevin said.

The sea was creeping slowly in. It did not move in one even sweep; hollows and channels unexpectedly seemed to have more water than a moment before, but how the tide had reached a particular point wasn't always obvious to the eye. Nor did it flow smoothly over the river-bed; the mud just seemed wetter than before as if the water was rising inside it, dissolving it, causing its apparent disintegration. Or mud that still looked dry could not be; flocks of birds, as if they had all suddenly developed a distaste for wet feet, rose in the air and flapped distractedly up-river, and what they had been standing on was no longer solid and substantial, but suddenly part of the sea. The incoming tide was louder than the ebb, occasionally sucking and dribbling, creating miniature whirlpools that sounded, briefly, like the gurgle of bath water. It's pleased, Cheryl thought; those are the noises of pleasure. It's happiest encroaching, entering the land. And the child, in birth, made the same journey, but out to sea.

"You still want to wallow in it?" Luke asked Aaron.

"Yes."

Chapter Seven

Cheryl gave birth to a daughter on October the twenty-second. She and Aaron had fallen out on every occasion when possible names for the child were mentioned, but eventually they agreed that if it was a girl Cheryl would decide, if a boy, Aaron. So the baby was called Rebecca Ruth. "How old-fashioned!" the clerk commented when Aaron went to register the birth, then, seeing his frosty expression, she added hastily, "I like the old-fashioned names best myself." Everyone in the Brown family was astonished that it was a girl; Doris, however, was not too displeased by the thought that she had a grand-daughter, and instantly started making plans for the christening. Peter checked up in the island's parish register and discovered that there had not been a Miss Brown for a hundred and two years. "A hundred and two years!" Doris repeated. "Just fancy that!" She, too, approved of the choice of Rebecca Ruth; Biblical names were undoubtedly the best; that was why she had chosen David, Aaron and Peter for her sons. Martin . . . well, that was Charlie's idea.

Luke had shown John the cottage at Roadwater, and he, too, had fallen in love with it. It was still on the market. They looked at other properties in the area, but knew they were not being serious. John offered a price and it was accepted. After that, the difficulties started. No building society would regard him, being self-employed, as a safe proposition unless he was prepared to put down a much larger deposit than he could afford. Luke's salary was not sufficient for him to be taken seriously either. The whole business made them both very angry; people like Jack and Kevin,

Luke reflected, would also be caught, in a variety of ways, in the same pitfalls. Eventually they obtained their mortgage, but only after Luke had persuaded the editor of his newspaper to make his income sound more generous than it was.

In fact, John's finances were not derisory. He had a lease on the pottery in London, and was able to sub-let it for a very good rent. Then, soon after moving to Somerset, he found a group of potters who were happy to let him share their studio; their fourth member had recently left the area. He did not know any of them but they had heard of him, and felt that his arrival would give them a certain cachet they had not previously had.

Their lives, soon after the move, began to revolve round the cottage. Going out in the evenings became unusual. Only when Cheryl came down to the estuary, as she did more often as winter passed and the weather turned warmer, did they make an effort and go out for the day. Sometimes Cheryl stayed at Roadwater. She and John got on well together. Luke was pleased at this; it meant that two different parts of his life could grow together harmoniously, or, as he admitted to himself in more candid moments, it eased his conscience. His relationship with Cheryl was as relaxed as it could ever be. The flare-up of emotion at her wedding had been dismissed by both of them as nonsense. They had come to look at each other as old friends; what had happened between them was past, buried. Though maybe not quite dead; somewhere inside Luke lay a niggling sense of dissatisfaction he was only occasionally aware of. It rose to the surface when the provincial backwater of his job depressed him and he would think of Aaron basking in his success. Something odd, surely, was going on there. Cheryl hardly ever visited the West Country with her husband. "He's working," she said, when Luke asked, and she would mention some distant place like Coventry or Leeds, but the expression on her face was, for a moment, unhappy or puzzled. Ron had resumed his career, of course. Not with the group; they had all gone their own ways. He was earning a reasonable amount of money, was busy cutting a new album: the pace was more congenial; Aaron superstar really was burned out. If it soon meant the Northern clubs or the universities on a Saturday night he didn't mind. Sometimes Luke thought he'd like to inflict some violence on Aaron: the man was neglecting his wife for his own selfish ends.

The cottage certainly needed attention. A new bathroom and

kitchen would soon be imperative, but that was beyond his abilities, and John's. Meanwhile they did what they could, tried to learn new skills – painting, carpentry, glazing – which was not easy for Luke, who was an extremely impatient person and wanted first-class results instantly. However, in six months they had laid a new floor upstairs, redecorated most of the rooms, re-rendered the whole of the outside, and put in bigger windows in the lounge. They removed the small brick fireplace and opened up the old hearth behind – discovering, in the process, an ancient bread-oven – and Luke stopped the fire smoking the room out by fashioning a hood from scrap metal. Undoubtedly the cottage was now less damp as a result of their efforts, more pleasant to live in: but as well as that, Luke was beginning to find a hitherto unknown satisfaction from this work, as if his thwarted creative impulses had been given vent at last and were shaping a work of art all round him. It was a physical satisfaction too: a bath had never been more gorgeous as he soaked out the ache from his back; or his hands, sore and cut from an excess of hammering or mixing concrete, softened. Plans chased each other in his head: they would eventually tackle the bathroom and kitchen, lay out the garden properly (at the moment it was a wilderness of dockweeds and stinging nettles), create a paradise.

His twenty-third birthday: he felt he had arrived somewhere at last. Manhood, maturity he supposed, though the words sounded a bit strange; he wasn't used to applying their meaning to himself. Eighteen months ago he had been a student worried by the approach of exams, penniless, his personal life a wretched mess of drinking and tom-catting that had led to gonorrhoea: now he had a lover, a job, a house. The ease with which it had happened! It couldn't last, this luck; there must be a down-turn, and soon: fortune's wheel. But why not rejoice, all the same, in the here and now? It was not every day one was twenty-three. He walked up to the winding-house, still his favourite place in Somerset, despite his discovery in recent months of the Quantocks and the coast between Lynmouth and Porlock, areas which were more immediately striking in their beauty. Up here he was king. It was a day similar to that first, a year ago, when he had watched the procession of clouds march towards him over the Bristol Channel and he had been captivated by the pattern of soft rounded hills dropping away to the sea. Zadok the priest and Nathan the prophet anointed Luke king!

But would it last? He still felt at times that his love for John was an aberration, an experience on the road to something else, just as this return to the West of England was a deviation from his real destiny, which was in London. Even the house on which he worked so lovingly he felt was more John's than his; John's was the sole name on the deeds, and, perhaps significantly, Luke did not mind that. He was glad not to have the responsibility of being a property owner. Well, he said to himself as he walked back down the incline, the only thing to do was not to make too many long-term plans. Play it by ear.

It was a favourite expression of his, play it by ear. What it really meant was that he didn't like to think about anything too carefully, particularly other people's feelings.

In the autumn some parts of Blackheath were given over to rugby pitches; Kevin, one cold damp afternoon in October, stopped on his way home from school to watch the progress of a game. The previous fortnight had been exceptionally wet and the ground was a quagmire, but this did not deter the players; they grabbed for the ball or each other as enthusiastically as they would if the earth was dry, rolling in the mud without a care for the clammy cold smears left on their legs and faces and clothes. He was fascinated: mindless animals, all concentration on either the oval-shaped bit of leather or dragging each other into a writhing heap of bodies. Whatever was the point of it? It was not his own adolescent detestation of games that he was recalling to mind; all he'd felt then was a generalised dislike, a sense of inferiority because he was no good at something people were told to enjoy, an envy of those who were adept. That envy he'd confused at the time with sexual desire, but it was simply a wish to be what he could never be, understandable enough at fifteen or sixteen, when he felt that Kevin, open and honest, would not be commendable to most of his peers and the adults of his life. The sense of shame and guilt which accompanied that self-knowledge drove him to try, unsuccessfully, to be what he was not, but when he began to learn to accept who he was, the envy slowly faded, and so did his desire for love or friendship or sex with teenagers who were hearty all-male youths.

Certainly nothing about the men he was watching seemed

sexually attractive. Even the one obviously good-looking youth, a tall lanky blond, failed to stir him, despite the very long legs and very short shorts, which were frequently and unnecessarily hitched up so that the creases under the bottom were visible and the ample bulge at the front was proudly emphasised: I'm a beautiful animal with a great big weapon, the youth seemed to be signalling to anyone who was interested; I'm not a person with a mind or feelings, all I'm created for is to chase leather balls, to wallow in mud, and to fuck. Even the language he and the others were using was stripped to a basic grunting mode of communication: "Pass, Dave, pass, pass!" "Back, Steve, back!" "Here, Kev! Kev, Kev, Kev!" So the blond youth had the same name as he did, and yet he did not: it had been reduced, like David and Stephen, to a monosyllable, as if it was just fancy decoration, too much effort to say it properly. And the swearing was not how he or Jack would swear, though the words were the same; they were explosions of real aggression, not bits of colour or emphasis as he might use them, but were of the same venom as words like queer or faggot uttered by straight yobbos who occasionally wandered into a gay pub, youths who strangely preferred to spend a Saturday evening mocking at gays instead of dancing with women. They're possibly gay themselves, people said: they're either unable to come to terms with it or else bisexuals ashamed of what might be considered a slur on their masculinity; one ought to feel sorry for them. But neither he nor Jack considered it prudent to spend time offering pity.

Perhaps they all had something in common with the rugby players here. So much physical contact: pulling another man down into the mud was a licence to touch which was not normally allowed. Maybe, really, they did need to experience the feel of another body of the same sex, and this was the only outlet they could permit themselves.

Luke and Aaron had talked, more than once in the summer, of fighting in the estuary. They'd had opportunity enough, but they had not taken advantage of it. Aaron did not seem so keen now as Luke, possibly because he feared he would be the loser, though a more likely reason was vanity: Aaron, Kevin guessed, did not relish the thought of hurt to his body, not necessarily because of the pain so much as the risk of cosmetic damage. It was not a simple matter of jealousy over Cheryl, but a need for some further revelation of the one to the other: they had loved and lived with the same girl, shared with her all their emotions, instincts, mental processes. Did they need to touch in consequence, to find answers they could not work out in any other way? Certainly they could read each other at a social level. But that did not unlock secrets each perhaps wanted to know; why they had both loved her, what it was she had found in them. Nor did it solve problems like which was the superior as a lover, as a companion, as a whole person. Really they ought to get into bed together, Kevin thought, for there they would find some of the answers.

Miss Sullivan's Advice Column, he said to himself as he walked away. Jack registered some amusement when Kevin told him what had been going through his mind. "I play games, too," he said.

"But that's only squash!"

"What do you mean, *only* squash?"

"There's no physical contact with other people, except by accident. All your aggression goes into the poor old ball."

"I don't feel particularly aggressive when I'm playing."

"Luke does."

"Yes, and that's both a strength and a weakness. He can hit the ball with tremendous speed, as hard and fast as I've ever seen. But not always accurately."

"Is he really very good?"

"Yes . . . but I don't think he would ever have been world class. Too impatient. And like your rugby players, a bit too animal. He plays every time as if he needs to wear himself into the floor. Games, my love, are more than just bodies, whatever you may think."

"He looks like a Mexican bandit these days."

"What do you mean?"

"That moustache he's grown."

"It looks like a copy of Aaron's. Perhaps it's some kind of uniform. I vant to be a clone! Anyway . . . John is very into macho men. What's to eat tonight?"

"Soufflé."

"We had that last Thursday, and the Thursday before." Jack smiled mischievously. "We're not falling into a life of habit and routine, are we?" Things had been restored so well that they were able to discuss last autumn without wounding each other; they could even joke about it.

"We probably are," Kevin said.

"Does it matter?"

"I don't know."

"It doesn't matter to me, but you aren't sure."

"No."

"Oh?"

"I'm never sure of anything, except that there's you and I'm not going to let *that* change. But . . . moods."

"Of?"

"Wanting excitement, I suppose. Whatever it was that produced last autumn hasn't just gone away."

"What shall we do then? Tonight. Where shall we go?"

"Nothing special."

Jack laughed. "I thought you said you were restless."

"I didn't mean now, at this minute. Anyway, it's too dark and gloomy to go out. Shall we invite Cheryl and Ron down later? Not mark exercise books for once."

"And afterwards? When they've gone?"

"I see." Kevin smiled. "It sounds as if it will be the usual sort of evening."

Although Rebecca's birth was normal in every way, Cheryl suffered acutely from post-natal depression. She did not realise quite how serious it was until she got home from the hospital, when, unable to open a window that had swollen in the damp weather, she deliberately smashed the glass with her fist. The resulting blood and bandages did not improve matters. That first evening in the flat she finished reading a novel she had begun in hospital, a story of adolescent love that ended tragically. *Fireweed* it was called. It made her weep floods of tears, and she begged Ron to take the book away, throw it in the dustbin, do anything he liked to get rid of it so long as it was out of the house. He couldn't, he protested; it was a library book. What on earth was wrong with her? She threw it at him.

He sought shelter downstairs.

"Baby blues," Kevin said. "My sister almost went dotty."

"Well, what the fuck am I supposed to do about it?"

"Don't talk to her like that!"

They glared at each other. "Ron, what's bothering you?" Jack asked.

"I don't know." He sat down, full of gloom.

"Shall I go and see her?" Kevin suggested.

"Please. Look . . . I'm sorry, Kevin. But I'm just bewildered!"

She was still crying. He lay on the sofa and held her in his arms. "It's time for women," he said. "You and me together. It takes another girl to understand."

She laughed, and kissed him. "Darling Kevin! You're not another girl."

"No, thank God! I was trying to joke you out of crying."

"I don't know what I'd do without you."

"You only have to call and I'll come."

"I know." She wriggled closer to him. "I should have married *you.*"

"Oh yes? I might do for the tea-and-sympathy department, but we'd never have had the baby in the first place. Now would we?"

She laughed again, muffled, into his sweater. "You never know."

"I bloody do! And my sweater's all wet. Look, if you don't stop crying soon, I'll start. I will, really. Shall I make you a coffee?"

"Please."

An hour later Aaron came in, and Kevin returned downstairs. "Did Ron talk?" he asked Jack.

"Yes. He can't cope. Can't cope at all."

"Why not?"

"He's somehow rejected the baby, I think. The fact that she's a girl doesn't help; God knows why. I can't understand it. What difference does it make? Maybe it's deeper; he can't regard himself seriously as a father, perhaps. Or can't bear the thought of Cheryl as a mother. You know Ron. He seemed content with the idea of giving up being the nation's number-one teenager, but now it's actually happened he's found nothing inside himself to help him be an ordinary adult. Aaron paterfamilias: he doesn't like it."

"He'll have to!"

"Or he'll have big butch Kevin after him?"

"Too bloody right he will! I've no time for him. None!"

Cheryl insisted on having the baby's cot beside her that night, and when Rebecca's crying woke Aaron from a deep sleep in the small hours of the morning, he felt, as she placed the child on their bed to change the nappy, an overwhelming desire to let rip with his feet and send his daughter hurtling through the window. I begin to understand the battered baby syndrome, he thought.

The crying disturbed Kevin and Jack. "Do you think they're all right?" Kevin asked.

"Of course! With you for a nurse they've got it made! You'll find all your need for excitement fulfilled now."

"Don't mock." He snuggled closer. Jack's lovely warm smell. "I can hear your heartbeat." He stroked the blond hair.

"Not now."

Kevin giggled. "I didn't mean that." He said, after thinking a while, "I wish we had one."

"One what?"

"One baby."

Jack laughed for so long that the bed shook. "What would you call it? Jemima?"

"Tabitha."

"Zachariah."

"I think the kid's . . . gorgeous!"

"So do I. And so are you." He laughed again. "You're so *sweet!*"

In the morning Aaron was sufficiently thoughtless to tell Cheryl of what had passed through his mind when she was changing the nappy. She was horrified. All that day and the next she was ridiculously protective to the baby, not leaving her alone with Ron for a second. "I said I could understand it, that's all!" he shouted. "It's a long way off doing it!" She said nothing, did not even look at him. He stormed out of the flat, slamming the door.

He had not exactly rejected the child, but she was undoubtedly a nuisance, a disruption to the peaceful routine of his home; she was the origin, too, of changes in his wife that he could not fathom: depression, hostility towards him. What Aaron did not understand he tended to brush aside, nor did he possess the humility to recognise his own part in the causes of unhappiness. The baby was Cheryl's business, not his. If Rebecca woke him he did not stir; Cheryl fed her, washed her, looked after all her needs. These were women's affairs; if he went out to work and brought home the money, played with the child in his free time (which he did), that was his part of the bargain discharged. He was often away for a night or two, sometimes longer; he had to be: he would return with expensive presents for both of them, but he was often greeted by Cheryl with less than warmth. Sometimes the baby smiled when he held her in his arms or dandled her on his knee, and he liked that, but it was inadequate compensation for a wife who was always down in the dumps and unresponsive in bed. She hardly ever seemed to want him these days, sexually. He tried to explain to her how frustrated he was, that he hadn't had such rotten sex since he was about fifteen: she replied that she could not help it. Eventually she went to the doctor, who put her on anti-depressants.

The pills made her sleepy all day long; he escaped downstairs and poured out his troubles. But Jack had no magic cure to offer; "Give her time" was all the advice he could give. Jack could see quite well how much larger was Aaron's role in causing the problem than Aaron could himself, but he did not think it useful to say so. Our superstar was hardly the kind of man who would take home-brewed marriage guidance from a homosexual.

It was Kevin more than anyone else who stopped Cheryl going completely off the rails. He took days off school to help her with the housework; sometimes at nights, when Aaron was away, he slept in the empty half of her bed. He loved the baby; "It's mine," he often said. "Baby B." (B was the ultimate diminutive of Rebecca, arrived at via Becky, then Beck.) Certainly she smiled and gurgled whenever he came near; more, he thought, than she did with her father. "Has he noticed that?" he asked Jack. "Does it matter?" Jack answered. Cheryl appointed him the child's honorary godparent. She was trying to fight off the pressure from her mother-in-law to have the baby taken to the island to be christened. "Just an excuse for Doris to parade herself in front of her neighbours," she said to Kevin. "She wants to show them how superior she is in having such a devoted family." However, if Doris won the battle, which was unlikely, perhaps Kevin would do the honours at the font. "Apart from anything else," Cheryl said, "it would annoy her, and I'd like that. She probably thinks she's got David or Peter already lined up for the job."

Though he would have done so to please Cheryl, Kevin was not at all keen on the idea of starring in a ritual he considered even more of a meaningless piece of mumbo-jumbo than most Christian ceremonies. All that nonsense about casting out devils! In the end he did not have to; Cheryl was adamant, and Doris, for once, did not get her own way. Ron was totally indifferent, of course, helping neither side in the argument. His mother was mightily put out, and said so at length to anyone who cared to listen.

Aaron watched the intimacy between Cheryl, Kevin and the baby with some sourness. He preferred, however, to nurse the grievance rather than do anything about it. At least it made Cheryl happier, and it relieved him a little of tiresome responsibilities. Let them get on with it, he thought. If Kevin was so soppy and wet that he preferred to play at being a girl, well, that was his affair. The trouble with Kevin, he decided, was that he was born in the wrong gender. Jack, Ray, and Tim, he had to admit, were not like that. Preferring a partner of one's own sex must, he thought, be unsatisfactory; it was a second-rate substitute for failing to achieve – for unknown, unknowable reasons – a proper desire for women. But Kevin, in his view, wanted to *be* a woman: that was crazy.

When Rebecca was six months old things were still far from satisfactory. Cheryl found she was often in low spirits, weepy, sometimes unable to face even the simplest tasks. She decided to go and stay with her parents for a month or two, maybe longer. Aaron protested, threatened, pleaded, but to no avail. When she had gone and he was alone he wondered if she would ever come back. He felt utterly lost. He was no villain, but he had always got more or less what he wanted, particularly since his teenage years, when his nature, limited anyway in its ability to sympathise or to be interested beyond ordinary curiosity in the operations of minds and hearts unlike his own, had been rendered more selfish by success. So, more than most, he was struck helpless by what was happening, and, incapable of seeing why, he could not discover any obvious path to follow which might retrieve the situation. All he could think of was that he had been badly and unreasonably hurt.

The editor from time to time hinted that Luke was too large a fish to spend his whole life swimming in the pond of this particular paper. Had he ever thought of television? The nationals? News agencies? Yes, Luke answered, he had certainly thought of them. One morning the editor told him that one of the bigger news agencies needed a man at their London office; an important person there, an old friend of his, had mentioned it. He could put in a word: think about it.

"Out of the question, of course," Luke said to John.

"But you would like it."

"I'm quite content."

"Oh no, you're not! I know you! How long are you going to be happy working for a dull provincial paper that has more misprints than the *Guardian*?" Luke was silent. "Women's Institute meeting at Stogumber. Dunster man fined for speeding. County Council say no to proposed new bypass. Oh yes, the real front-page stuff of life." Luke stood up, searched for a record, and put on the Mozart *Requiem*. "I'm right, aren't I?"

"Stop it!"

"Farmers plough up four hundred acres of Exmoor each year."

"That does interest me."

"Not much you or your editor can do about it."

"Are you saying I ought to apply for this job?"

John sighed. "You'll do what you want to do. You always have done."

Quite different from the hushed distance of Verdi's opening, Luke thought, or Britten's harsh jangling bells. *Et lux perpetua*. A good recording, this. "You astound me," he said.

"Mens boglat?"

"One hundred per cent. Here, I have . . . everything."

"No one has that."

"Suppose I did. Don't you think it might put a strain on our relationship?"

"Maybe in the long run less."

"You're incredible." Luke paced up and down. Once an attractive proposition entered his head he always found it very hard to dismiss it. His mind had been whirling all day, ever since the editor had put the temptation in front of him. He'd hoped John would help him resist, but here his lover was, actively giving him encouragement! "Quite incredible!" he repeated. *Et lux perpetua luceat eis*. "What would we do? Sell up, move back to London?"

"No."

"No? What, then?"

"You go. I stay."

"No." He thought for a moment, then said in a rather hurt voice, "It sounds as if you actually want me to leave!"

"We've created this house. We're still creating it. It would be like cutting off an arm to sell it now! A rootless person – me – has grown roots. I'll *never* sell it. Never! You, I suppose, haven't grown into this place."

"That's not true! And you know it."

111

"The choice is clear."

"It isn't!" *Kyrie eleison, Christe eleison.* Severe Handelian fugue.

John relented, a little. "I wouldn't want you in London for good. But . . . for a while, yes, I could manage." He put on his jacket and picked up the car keys. "Look, I have to go to the pottery; the kiln's on."

Luke banged his fist on the table. "I said . . . what do I do?"

"There's no need to shout! I've given you my opinion, and there's no need to repeat it."

"You're a bastard."

"I'm not."

"Oh yes, you are! So calm and cold and calculating! Sometimes I loathe you!" He grabbed hold of the nearest object – an ash-tray that John had made – and threw it on to the floor. It broke in several pieces. They both stared at it for a moment without speaking, then looked at each other.

"Why don't you just . . . for once . . . stop thinking about yourself and consider how you fuck up other people's lives?" John went out, quietly shutting the door.

Tuba mirum spargens sonum! The solo trombone was something of a disappointment. Verdi's trumpets were the ultimate in blazing fire, the very essence of doomsday, but Mozart, coming before, could hardly be blamed for not having the basic technical resources at hand. Luke was on a Requiem crawl this week : Fauré, Verdi, Britten, Berlioz; this was the fifth. The Britten was excellent, but the Verdi supreme. It was one of the half-dozen most sublime works in all music.

Oh yes, what John was saying was ridiculous. And somewhat unpleasant, to say the least. Yet only last week Luke had had an extremely uneasy day. He'd been watching *News at Ten* the night before, and there, amazingly, was an item from an eager young reporter, Owen, of all people, Owen Crawley! What the *fuck* was he doing there? What qualifications, what contacts did he have to be standing in Glasgow, telling the nation that an elderly storekeeper had died in a distillery fire? Owen Crawley . . . *News at Ten* . . . Glasgow. Luke seethed with jealousy: that, more than anything he'd ever thought of, was what he'd like to do. Luke Edwards . . . *News at Ten* . . . Mogadishu. (Or Athens, Luang Prabang, Caracas). Our Man in Cambodia. (Perhaps not

Cambodia, on second thoughts.) He dashed out of the house and phoned Jack to find out how Owen had done it. But Jack knew nothing, had not seen the broadcast, thought his brother was operating a computer in Edinburgh. Why was Luke so interested?

Why was it he liked sacred music so much? It was odd, seeing that all his conscious life he had been an unbeliever, had found even the objective study of comparative religions at school very boring. All that absorption in futilities that only hindered man's happiness! Yet he was a devotee of motets,cantatas, masses, oratorios; anything from the *Great C Minor Mass* to *The Dream of Gerontius* held his attention as much as the simplest hymns in *Ancient and Modern* . . . casting down their golden crowns around the glassy sea. Perhaps the music was a kind of trigger, a catalyst, that made it possible to place the most powerful and irrational forces inside himself in some sequence or order, to show meaning in the most clashing of opposites, to make sense of it all in notes on a stave: *Rex tremendae majestatis, qui salvandos salvas gratis, salve me fons pietatis.* That was indeed a paradox, yet it rhymed, had the same sound.

It didn't help him to *resolve* his own paradoxes, but maybe it made them less important. For he loved John, hurried to be back with him at night, loved the intimacy of the cottage even when he was immersed in the immediate task of planing a piece of wood while his partner, equally absorbed, was reading a book or painting the window-sill : they were within calling distance, under the same roof, *their* roof. An image of his father came into his head. After Mum had died and Adam had left to go to the university, Dad and he lived rather like this. Two men sharing a house : a warm, comfortable silence. He put his hands over his face. There were still moments, thinking of his father, when he would shudder and find his eyes wet. "The bastard dying on me like that," he said, aloud. He had repeated those words a thousand times.

A confused murmur of voices in his head : office telephones ringing, challenges, assignments. A girl. Marriage. Children. He wasn't the sort of person who had ever considered that the primary function of his balls was to reproduce himself, but . . . girl's smooth skin, soft warm breasts : he'd almost forgotten the pleasure. But I owe him so much! *Too* much! He seems to *want* to break it up. Why? Does he fancy somebody else, somebody I don't even know, who's waiting patiently, who'll move in here the day I leave?

113

Of course not! That's madness! Equally mad to give up what I've got for a possible nothing. He's given me everything.

A few things he could do without, too. Pain recently, when urinating. He had gone to the doctor : venereal warts. He had made an appointment at the hospital to have them removed. A full anaesthetic – a cyst on his foreskin, which had been there for years, was also going to be dealt with – and that meant staying in overnight.

I love him. I can't leave him.

The second side of the record finished. He hadn't listened to any of it : *ne me perdas illa die*.

Owen Crawley!

114

Chapter Eight

It was several days before Cheryl could make herself tell her mother what it was that had brought her back to the farm, and even then she was very incoherent: she had little idea herself of what exactly had happened, except that the rift between her and Aaron was deeper than it appeared to be. She could not understand why she placed such weight on his remark about understanding people who battered their babies. She knew quite well that Rebecca was in no danger; Ron was not the kind of person who would work out his temper on an innocent little child. It was probably no more than the momentary irritation any parent might feel towards its offspring, but for Cheryl it made blindingly clear all the dissatisfactions she had ever felt about him, but which she had previously made light of, indeed at one time had thought were qualities, positively good reasons for marrying him.

Perhaps she was being very unfair. Certainly her mother seemed to think so, hinting that she was over-reacting to the ordinary problems of marriage, that post-natal depression always tended to make everything ugly and distorted.

"Post-natal depression!" Cheryl shouted. "I'm sick and tired of hearing that as an excuse for everything! The baby's six months old!"

Mrs Wood sighed. "You're not giving him a chance."

"I just want to recover," she said, wearily. "I thought maybe down here it was possible. I want to go back; I've every intention of going back. It's . . . just something inside me I've got to sort out."

"Do you love him?" She did not answer. "Cheryl. Can I say . . . well, it might be a clue."

"Go on."

"Luke."

"What about him?"

"You loved him. That I *know*. It's never been quite the same with Ron, has it?" She stared out of the window, refusing to meet her mother's eyes. "Maybe that's your answer."

"I'm not still in love with Luke, if that's what you mean."

"I meant Aaron was . . . he caught you on the rebound."

"Perhaps." And perhaps she did see Luke too much in terms of a novelette hero, she decided. She took the baby out for a walk, wheeling the pram along the road towards Quintin's Man. This landscape, every corner of it, had associations with Luke. It was a mild spring day, but on the moor the changes of the seasons came late. There was little sign of things growing, new grass or fern-heads, only the sombre dead vegetation of winter, last year's weeds and copper bracken dulled by months of frost, snow and rain. Great Kneeset, High Willhays, Yes Tor filled much of the sky with their dark beetling slopes and rocky summits. She seemed particularly aware today (maybe it was something to do with the light) of the vast number of boulders, mostly near the peaks, or resting on the hillsides, in the stream, on level ground. They looked as if they had been scattered at random by a giant who had picked up the remains of a mountain smashed in some cosmic quarrel and hurled them into the places where they now lay. Up here one was free, Luke had once said: today, though, it was depressing. The last great wilderness, people often called Dartmoor; wilderness aptly described it. She intensely disliked the power it had to make her feel so tiny.

By the bridge, she remembered Luke throwing stones and making rude comments about tourists who parked their cars in the passing places. She saw him larger than he was, a giant, striding about the moor searching for her lost horse (a clumsy boy's attempt, in fact, to chat her up) or helping her father to erect a fence: in no time at all, it seemed, the fence was built, firm, solid, and lasting. Aaron would wither in such surroundings: obsolescent packaged plastic man, not capable of growth, only of deterioration.

Next day she drove to Somerset and the brief hour or two she had thought to spend with Luke and John lengthened to three days. It was images of growth she was constantly made aware of here, in the cottage, the countryside. Winter had disappeared altogether. The grass was lush; primroses flowered in the hedges; everywhere buds covered branches and looked, at a distance, like a film of green dust. The cottage garden, which John had now partly cleared, was a mass of fresh colour: under the tangle of nettles and blackberries he had discovered daffodils, hyacinths, crocuses. A forsythia dazzled against the wall. From the farm just along the road there came a perpetual murmur of young creatures: lambs, calves; four dogs not much beyond puppyhood who streaked out when people passed, gambolling, barking. John, Luke, and the house seemed woven together into one organic living thing although the separate parts held the attention of the others – became, momentarily, the focal point – Luke serving up dinner, John making a niche in one of the cob walls for three of his pots, both of them laying lino tiles or fooling around in the kitchen. Each of the parts was so dependent on the others, so much fused with them, that Luke's announcement that he was going to work in London struck Cheryl as bizarre in the extreme, an impossibility almost. Also quite unnecessary: when something a little like perfection had been reached, why destroy it? She remembered one of Luke's favourite quotations:

> And that this place may thoroughly be thought
> True Paradise, I have the serpent brought.

What was this particular serpent? she wondered. Maybe what they had achieved was itself the trouble. One always had to move on.

They spent an afternoon at Blue Anchor collecting stones, strange black things, blacker than any rock Cheryl had ever seen before on a beach and almost perfectly smooth, and pieces of alabaster: in the cliffs it looked as exotic as fancy decoration on the side of a cake, and crushed and broken in her hand it reminded her of pink coconut ice. John found three pieces of shale stained a dullish green. He took them home and placed them in an old coffee jar which he filled with water: the green became vivid, the colour of a wet field.

"What are they?" Cheryl asked.

"I don't know." He was trying to find out from an old geology book. "It looks like some deposit. Copper perhaps, or arsenic."

"Arsenic!" Luke exclaimed. He picked up the jar and put it on the highest shelf, well out of Rebecca's way.

Even stones have secrets, Cheryl thought, enough to absorb the three of them for a whole afternoon. The cliffs at Blue Anchor with their strata of different rocks packed and stacked tight together were an X-ray of what, inland, was under the land, an exposure of its nerves, bones and sinews, such as was never possible to see of people. For some unknown reason this idea impelled her into speech, and she found she was telling the others the events of her life since the baby's birth, analysing them aloud in a manner far more coherent than she had previously been capable of. Luke kept his anger to himself, but his face flushed as he thought of what he would like to do to Aaron: the one-time premier sound of the nation sprawled in Exe mud. "Come and stay with us whenever you want," he said. "We've had the phone put in now, but you don't have to ring. Just come." He put his arms round her and kissed her.

The following day they drove to Glastonbury. They explored the abbey ruins and sat under the holy thorn, eating a picnic lunch. Luke snapped a twig off the tree and slipped it into his pocket.

"Abbot Whiting will haunt you for that," John said.

"I shall plant it in the garden when we get home."

"And, as it did for Joseph of Arimathea, it will bloom instantly, I suppose."

"It flowers on Christmas Day, doesn't it?" Cheryl asked. "Don't they send a piece of it to the Queen?"

"Pardon me, ma'am," Luke said, giggling, "but can I have my staff back?"

Later, they climbed Glastonbury Tor, Luke lugging Rebecca in his arms. The flat ground of the top was a sea of mud and dung, the medieval church tower rising up like an island castle in the middle. Several cows stood there, staring at them. "Perhaps they can't get down, poor things," John suggested. "It's ferociously steep."

"It's where old cows come to die," Luke said. "The weirdos who watch the sun at midsummer. They've all been transmogrified."

"What weirdos?" Cheryl asked.

"They believe this place has cosmic vibrations. And they meet Circe who turns them into cows."

"Sows, that was," John said. "Any cosmic vibrations, Cheryl?"

"No. But the view's good."

It was easy to understand why Glastonbury must have seemed like an island, Luke thought, the Isle of Avalon. All around the flat Somerset fields stretched like a green sea to the foot of the distant hills, Mendips, Poldens, far-off Quantocks. Wells cathedral, minute but clear, stood at the sea's edge. All incredibly ancient. The dawn of civilisation; it had to be here: man's imagination flares in such places, makes connections, finds meaning. No wonder it was soaked in myth and legend. A ship on a green sea. Of course there was a simple boring scientific explanation, faults and fissures, lesser oolites or greensand or something. But the special charge was not simple: the fusion of landscape and imagination, perceived again and again over the centuries.

He stayed up there for some time after John and Cheryl had started to scramble down. "Hey!" he cried. "Hey!"

They stopped and turned. He was a black silhouette, the sun behind him. He stood, legs apart, a giant; or a star, Cheryl thought, a black star, arms, legs and head five black rays. He lifted Rebecca up, as if he was offering the child to the sun. "Stupid berk!" John muttered.

"I'm the king!" he cried. "And Rebecca is the heir to my kingdom!"

I shall find some way to leave him, John said to himself. I can't stand him any longer: he is such a child!

Luke caught up with them, all energy and excitement. "Did you receive the vibrations?" he asked.

"We saw a melodramatic fool."

"I was sending out vibrations." He laughed. "You did feel them," he said, completely mistaking the expression in John's eyes.

Jack often thought Kevin had the easier job as a teacher. Instilling rudimentary French into recalcitrant teenagers whose minds were understandably more interested in sex and football than la France, sa langue, sa vie, ses coutumes, was something quite soul-destroying. Kevin's enthusiastic primary-school kids, working out their Fletcher maths, or turning milk-bottle tops and toilet rolls into dragons and daleks, were a much more attractive prospect. He was often too tired to want to stir out of his chair, but Kevin seemed to have bouts of frenetic energy, cleaning the flat and reorganising the furniture.

He arrived home one evening surprised to find the table laid for four and Kevin busy in the kitchen. The mixer was whirring; all the burners were in use; every saucepan had something bubbling in it, or was waiting to be washed up. "A good cook uses everything in sight," he said when Jack complained about the pile of dirty pots and dishes.

"What's all this for?"

"You haven't forgotten?" He paused, looking slightly exasperated. "Ray and Chris are coming to dinner."

"Oh. Yes." Jack had forgotten. They'd met Ray by chance at a party a few weeks ago, the first time they'd seen him since Cheryl's wedding. They had spent most of the evening together talking of mutual friends they discovered they knew, Ray's job (he worked for a publisher), his passion for Spain and all things Spanish. Come to dinner, he said, and suggested a date. The meal was cooked by the young blond dance student he lived with: tonight was the return invitation. It was an episode that had left Jack slightly uneasy. He'd been aware that Ray and Kevin had found each other attractive, and that Chris, who was a sweet, quiet lad, and superbly good-looking despite being dressed in knee-length boots, old jeans and a tatty muslin garment that vaguely resembled a shirt, was often looking at him with the sort of expression that seemed to say "if" or "perhaps" or even "when?". Later, on their own, Jack discussed all this with Kevin, who had experienced the same unease, and also a similar kind of mild excitement; but in the next few days, involved in other things, they had thought no more about it.

Jack helped himself to some wine. "Don't drink too much of that," Kevin warned. "There isn't a lot, and they may not bring a bottle." Sainsbury's Minervois: the usual plonk, quite pleasant. Why was it, even in the best and most stable relationships, there was always a desire to explore outside? There seemed to be nothing wrong between Ray and Chris; they had lived together for about a year, and, like himself and Kevin, were obviously content with their shared life, possessions, interests. The price paid for stability was lack of surprise, and existence that wasn't necessarily humdrum, but . . . predictable. Even in bed. Happily so, of course, for ninety-nine per cent of the time. It was that other one per cent.

The phone rang. The mental picture of Chris vanished as Jack recognised his mother's voice. "I just wondered how you were," she said.

"Oh . . . er . . . we're having some people to dinner," he answered, momentarily flustered.

"How's Kevin?"

"Oh, he's fine." The question was unexpected: what was going on?

"Jack . . . your father's going to be away for a long weekend at the beginning of July. Some conference for bank managers; did you ever hear of such a thing? What on earth do they want to confer about?"

"Overdrafts, I imagine."

"Look . . . I shall be on my own here. Would you like to come down and stay?" He hesitated. "Both of you, that is."

"Why . . . yes! . . . I don't know what to . . . what's happened?"

"It's just . . . time, that's all." At last! At last! "Isn't the weather dismal?" she went on, glad to be on safer ground. "All our spring flowers smashed with this rain. You'd think it was November, and in a fortnight's time it will be flaming June!"

Kevin, absorbed in the intricacies of chicken véronique, did not instantly respond to Jack's delight and pleasure. "About time too," was his only comment.

"It's half the battle."

"The easier half."

"But you'll come?"

"Of course." The prospect did not thrill him very much. A long weekend with Mrs Crawley in that damp old house near the edge of the moor was not likely to be a great deal of fun.

The dinner-party was similar to the evening at Ray's, the same atmosphere. The wine did run out (perhaps they'd drunk more rapidly than usual, considering the circumstances); Jack decided to go to the pub and buy some more. "I'll come with you," Chris offered.

"It's all right."

"No, let me get this bottle. Please."

"We'll wash up while you're out," Kevin said. Activity in the kitchen was less dangerous than sitting next to Ray on the sofa.

"You're a good cook," Ray said, as he dried the dishes. "Kevin . . ."

"Yes?"

He smiled. "You know."

Kevin looked at him with what he hoped was a calm, level gaze, though he was not feeling particularly calm. Why did this have to occur? In nearly every gay relationship both partners eventually

121

did so; most of them said it helped to keep them together. Was it so necessary? It hadn't worked for him and Jack. And here was the possibility of moving towards the same disaster as before. They'd recovered, picked up the pieces, but a second time would be extremely difficult. Why are gays so promiscuous, he remembered Aaron asking, and Jack going on about the pressures of society. Kevin thought there was a lot of truth in his lover's comment. But Ray was beautiful. Dark skin, dark eyes. A warm, easy person. And Jack was a long time in the pub with Chris; were they planning something? If he did, should he tell Jack? It ought not to affect them at all, he thought; a few hours with somebody else just for the sake of a change should not produce traumas; what they had should not be so fragile that someone like Ray would break it. And it wasn't fragile; of that he was certain. Jack didn't own him, nor he Jack; neither of them had the right to make a prisoner of the other's sexuality any more than any other aspect of their lives and personalities. Possessiveness, jealousy: that was fragility in a relationship.

No! It wouldn't do. "I love Jack," he said.

"But . . ."

"But nothing. I love him."

"I want to. Very much."

Kevin shook his head. "No!"

Ray kissed him. "Phone me some time."

Aaron concentrated on his work. He had rehearsals with a group, some engagements in London clubs, discussions with an advertising agency about a soft drinks commercial; nothing exceptionally strenuous, but he was too busy to take a holiday which was what he thought he should do. He felt ridiculous, the deserted husband, a figure that was pathetic to the people who knew. It was as if Cheryl had written on his face, plain for them to see, the word "inadequate". He wished he could hide from Jack and Kevin, and he was off-hand, almost rude, to them when they asked if he was all right, did he need a meal cooked, should they do his laundry or go out for his shopping? Of course he wanted her back. He looked such a fool without her. Surely they could start again, recapture what it had been like at its best; surely he would learn to love the presence of the baby. But she . . . she was so changed; this depressed defensive creature, so protective of her

122

child, nudging him away, pushing him out: why? Why had it happened?

Af first he rang her daily, sometimes more than once. He thought he sounded reasonable and convincing in these phone conversations; it was easier to make the right sort of approach not being with her face to face, speaking without an excess of pleading, without anger, the all-loving, concerned, only slightly aggrieved husband. "I want you here. And soon. That's for sure."

"I haven't gone in that sense."

"I'm terrified you have."

"As soon as I've sorted myself out I'll be home."

"What is there to sort out?" Silence. "How's Rebecca?"

"Fine."

Silence. "I'm longing to see her. And you. Shall I come down?" Silence. Then, wearily, "All right," and, trying to sound as he had when he thought it was so natural that he'd not been forced to think about how to say it, "I love you."

"I love you too." But her voice was wrong: false, uncertain.

"Do you? You did, yes." Silence. "I'll phone tomorrow."

Should he go down there and drag her away? That was what Luke would do. He could easily imagine Luke riding off, like a knight in shining armour, the girl – or would it now be a boy? – flung across the horse's back, but when he substituted himself in the picture it was totally absurd. Ignore her, make no contact for five or six days? See if he cared. Wouldn't she worry about him then, try and reach Jack or Kevin to find out if all was well? Didn't she wonder if he was eating properly, or had a change of clean underclothes; wasn't she concerned that he might have another girl in the flat, or be maimed in a terrible accident? In hospital? Dead? It seemed not.

His manager said something about the possibility of a trip to America. Aaron dismissed the idea; it was hardly the appropriate time when he had so many personal problems. He was mad, Ricky said over and over again; it was the opportunity of a lifetime: think about it. Aaron began to think about it. The experience. The money. He tried to discuss it with Cheryl, but she didn't appear to mind whether he went or not. He wouldn't decide, he said, until she returned. Maybe she could come with him, she suggested. That hadn't entered his calculations: the problems of Cheryl and Rebecca on an American tour; how did you cope with a neurotic wife and a little baby on a series of one-night engagements in California? "I don't know whether it's possible," he said, cautiously. She rang off. "God damn and blast it all!" he shouted to the empty flat, and, furiously angry, went out and got paralytically drunk. The next night, after the gig, he took one of the girls home. It was exactly how he liked sex: no strings of any sort, almost anonymous, just bodily pleasure. It hadn't been like that for years. A few days later he signed a contract which would take him to America for two months.

The afternoon he packed he heard someone come into the house, and, assuming it was Kevin home from school, he went downstairs to tell him he would be away for a while, and please cancel the milk and the papers; keep an eye on things. He was surprised to find Luke, who explained that he was about to start a new job; he was going to sleep on Kevin's sofa for a few days until he found a place of his own.

"What's happened?" Aaron asked. "You haven't suffered the same problems as me, I hope."

"We aren't all like you!"

"Don't you start making judgements!"

Luke paused. "I'm sorry. About everything. Including what I just said; it's none of my business."

"No. But . . . if you're wanting somewhere to stay, you might as well go upstairs." And he told Luke about the trip to America.

"When's Cheryl due back?"

"I don't know. You can sort something else out then, I suppose."

"Well . . . thanks." He was grateful. "What about the rent?"

"Oh, nonsense! I doubt if you'll be here that long. And . . . would you do me a favour? Give this letter to Cheryl when you see her."

"Why don't you post it to the farm?"

"I'd rather it waited till she was here."

"Ok. And . . . thanks."

That evening Aaron was in a jumbo, talking excitedly with his manager, with the musicians who were travelling with them, his inside a nervous jumble of butterflies: the danger of aeroplanes, the immediate future a question-mark. It was a long time since he had experienced the pleasures of setting forth, and testing them again, he wondered how it was that he had been able to give them up so easily and gladly. It was a delight to find that old clothes still fitted.

If you want a separation, he had said in his letter, I shan't stand in your way. Financially you should be in a reasonable position. I'll arrange with the bank to pay you half of what is in my current account once a month. I intend to keep the house at Greenwich but I'll give you the cottage. I don't want it this way; I hope you still think there's a chance we can make a go of it. I shall come back at the end of July, and in the meantime you can write to me via Ricky Bernstein. What love I have for anybody is for you. Maybe you think it's a poor thing, but it's yours.

Now, on the plane, he almost wished she would decide on a separation. He was experiencing an enormous sense of release; distance was loosening him from ties he didn't want, perhaps had never really wanted. He couldn't reverse the process, make the plane turn round: it was all out of his control. He concentrated his thoughts on what lay ahead, the pleasure of beaches and sun, of singing and playing rock music, of congenial similar people, girls, parties: California would surely be something like what he'd always read about it.

Kevin and Jack leaned on the wall. The sun, now low behind Tower Bridge, flickered in the murky river. Cranes, warehouses: the Greenwich waterfront, deserted at this hour of the day. Barges clanked one against another. A hot summer evening in the grimy city. "It's been good just recently," Kevin said, throwing his cigarette end down into the mud.

"What has?"

"Us. I don't know why. It's just seemed particularly good. The theatre yesterday. And going into that shop to buy an aspidistra when all we wanted was a light-bulb. You've been . . . no, I can't explain it. Why are you frowning?"

"There's something I ought to tell you."

"What?"

"Christ. My heart's beating so fast it hurts."

Kevin felt for it. "Too many fags. Or is it what you're about to tell me?"

"It's not a joke."

"Oh?"

"Do you remember the Saturday evening after Ray and Chris

125

came to dinner? I went to the club for a game of squash."

"Vaguely."

"Well . . . Chris turned up there. I didn't know he was coming. And I did play squash; I wasn't lying. Then I . . . we . . . went into the park and . . ." Kevin's face was frozen. "Sweetheart." Jack kissed him. "I'm sorry. The trouble is . . . I don't regret it."

Kevin pulled away. "What . . . what does it imply?"

"Nothing."

"And I was thinking how good it had been."

"That's not a delusion! It hasn't been cancelled out! The only difference it's made to us is . . . I love you all the more."

"That's easily said." Kevin lit another cigarette, an almost unheard-of thing for him to do: he usually smoked no more than four or five in a week.

"But true. I couldn't have a relationship with Chris! I'd rather fly to the moon! I just found him there, that's all."

"Will it happen again?"

"It won't if you make me promise not to."

"But you wouldn't like me to force you into that."

There was a long silence. "Kevin. Does it really matter?"

It was difficult to think it out coherently. A number of conflicting emotions raced through him, but the sensations of anger and being hurt were lessened by the knowledge that he had wanted to go to bed with Ray, that Jack loved him to the exclusion of all other, that the love between them was not easily shaken and . . . yes, curiously, might not be damaged by this. "You've a speck of dirt on your face," he said, and rubbed it off with his forefinger.

"Kevin . . . I can't bear the idea of hurting you! But I can't hide something like that! I wish . . . I could say I feel bad I did so. I can't. I'm sorry. Smash my face in or something; I deserve it. You've been so loving these past few days and . . . well . . . I feel so guilty about . . . not feeling guilty."

"Wasn't it a bit cold on the grass?"

"Damp."

"Come to think of it, when I put your trousers in the washing-machine, I did wonder why they had green stains on them. Look . . . can we go back to the Yacht, please? I need another drink."

They walked along the tow-path in silence, Jack miserable, not daring to ask Kevin to say any more, but willing him to do so. Was their life together now wrecked? Kevin, aware of Jack's unhappiness, felt unable to anything about it; it required only a few words, just one sentence, but he could not bring himself to speak. Which was absurd and hateful, he thought, because it didn't matter, didn't matter at all.

Half-way through his beer he squeezed Jack's hand and said, "If it does happen again, just don't tell me."

"I love you."

"I know. And I love you."

Chapter Nine

Luke had been in London a month. He worked in ten-day shifts: afternoons and evenings; all night; then finally mornings and afternoons. After that he started on the afternoon and evening shift again. The work was entirely concerned with the collection of news, turning it into presentable story and disseminating it to newspapers. He found it an exciting, rewarding existence; to be one of the first in the country to hear of a revolution in Bangladesh or the latest peace moves in Cairo, and to be responsible for presenting this information to people, was a lot more worthwhile than scooping a Women's Institute meeting in Minehead. Between each shift he had three days off, and he usually returned to Roadwater, where the absolute silence of the countryside contrasted so much with the noise of Fleet Street and Greenwich that sometimes he wondered if he had grown deaf.

There was silence, too, inside the cottage. John spoke to him in monosyllables, and only in answer to questions. This enraged Luke far more than any outright quarrel, and he worked out his frustration by smashing things, usually pieces of pottery John had made. "What in the name of fuck is eating you?" he yelled on one occasion. "Why are you making me behave like this?"

"I don't know."

"Do you want me to leave for good? Is that it?"

"You will if you want to."

"You will if you want to! You always say that! Well, I don't want to! You may own this house, name on the title deeds and all that. But it's my home too!"

"Is it?"

"Oh, for Christ's sake!"

They made love, however, as often as they had done in the past. But it was always violent now, without any tenderness, an expression, by both of them, of anger and hurt. "Suck me," Luke would say, pulling down his zip, and, forcing John to his knees and gripping his head, he would use his cock as if he was trying to push it out of the back of his lover's neck. John never resisted. I suppose he still thinks it's the ultimate in giving, Luke said to himself, contemptuously.

One day after he had returned to Greenwich, he was sitting on the window-seat in the flat, staring out at the view. It was raining, a thin fine drizzle more commonly seen in the West Country than in London; he could pick out all the glass rods of it separately, so that he was not always certain which was rain and which were the shrouds of the Cutty Sark in the distance below. The columns of wet dragged up-river, darkening the hills across the city. At least the money's a bloody sight better, he said to himself; he had bought a washing-machine for the house at Roadwater and rented a television. Divine consumer durables! Were they to be the chief end-product of his work? And why did Aaron and Cheryl have no decent records? He missed his own; Radio Three was no substitute. He hummed the theme of 'Being Beauteous' from Britten's *Les Illuminations:* overtly gay love songs, Jack had once said. They had the record downstairs, of course. It was a masterpiece of the first order. I must get out of the habit of saying that, he told himself, thinking of all the music he'd called a masterpiece of the first order in the last few weeks, the Elgar cello concerto, Stravinsky's *Symphony in Three Movements, Fingal's Cave, The Swan of Tuonela, Die Winterreise,* the Vaughan Williams fourth, even things that patently weren't masterpieces, like bits of Dvorak and Mahler or Rodrigo's *Concierto de Aranjuez.*

The door opened, startling him. It was Cheryl. "What the hell are you doing here?" she asked, taking in at a glance that he wasn't a casual visitor, but had evidently been living in the flat for some while. He explained. She didn't seem to mind. "I'm dead beat," she said flopping down in a chair. "That journey! Rebecca was a blasted nuisance all the way, then just as we arrived in London she went to sleep."

"I'll make you a cup of tea."

"Please."

And later, glad to be of use, he cooked a meal for them both, heated tins of food for the baby and fed her. Cheryl watched him, pleased with the attention he gave to Rebecca, who was now crawling all over the place at a reckless speed, her little fingers into everything.

"Just like old times," he said, as they ate in the kitchen.

"Not exactly," she answered, rather tartly.

He smiled. "I must go soon. I'm working nights this week. And I'd better get my stuff together."

"What for?"

"You'll hardly want me here now. I'll move in with Kevin and Jack till I find somewhere."

"You can stay here if you like. There's room."

He stared at her. "Is it wise?"

"It's not likely to harm either of us, is it?"

"I don't know what to say."

"What would John think?"

"John? It hardly matters any more what he thinks."

It was very convenient, he kept saying to himself as he worked throughout the night. And obviously pleasant, no rent to pay; the kid would benefit from having a man about the house. When he returned to the flat at breakfast-time, all was quiet, Cheryl and the baby not yet stirring. He opened the bedroom door and looked at her.

"I'm just about to get up," she said, with a yawn. "You might as well climb in."

"That could be very silly." But, in bed, he turned away from her and fell asleep at once.

Inevitably of course, a few days later, they did make love, a gently affectionate experience that was also protective, even therapeutic. He had almost forgotten the pleasures of sleeping with a woman: exploring Cheryl's body was like the discovery of a marvellous new country. And it gave him the certain knowledge, as perhaps nothing else could have done, that he would never again think of Cheryl as the girl he should have married; the stupid emotions which had poisoned him on her wedding-day would never recur. As far as she was concerned a problem that had been worrying her considerably now seemed less important: that her sexuality had somehow been damaged, that she might not want to make love again. More than just that, of course: it was Luke, not any man; it was the final healing touch that cured old wounds.

It didn't happen often. Luke was determined not to take advantage when he felt frustrated and just wanted sex. It would ruin what they had achieved.

"Do you realise we've given Aaron grounds for divorce?" she said.

"I don't particularly care. Do you?"

"No."

"I shouldn't think he'll find out, anyway. Luke the co-respondent! A frisson I didn't think of at the time."

"Nor did I."

"What are you going to do about him?"

"I hope I shall want him back. I hope he'll want to come."

"Do you think it's likely?"

"Yes. As a matter of fact I do. I already feel clearer; the complex tangle is unknotting itself."

So is the tangle inside me, Luke said to himself. The next relationship he would have would be with a woman. His homosexuality, he decided, did not spring from instinct or emotion, but from the head: it had been an intellectual choice. Not a question of heart or genitals, but brain. He knew, however, that if he said something along those lines to Jack or Kevin, they would laugh at him and tear such woolly thinking to shreds. Anyway, he was in no hurry to rush out and settle for the first girl he saw : he wasn't yet quite ready to leave John altogether.

Kevin was jealous, Jack disapproving. Kevin had been usurped as Cheryl's comforter, the baby's chief playmate. "Kicked out by big bull Luke," he said. Jack argued that Kevin's role as nursemaid to Cheryl could only be a temporary affair anyway. "Yes," he answered bitterly. "I'm gay. I lose out again."

"That's silly. You see the baby almost as frequently as you did before."

But Kevin remained hurt. "There's only one difference. When I slept in her bed I stayed limp. It all comes back to that."

"We don't know that Luke doesn't."

"Don't be a fool!"

"Do you wish you hadn't?"

"No. Definitely not."

"I don't understand, then."

"I'm thinking of what *she* wants."

In a sense Jack's disapproval was moral; Cheryl, he thought, was being used so that Luke could yet again play macho man. He admitted he was exaggerating when Luke protested that it wasn't like that at all.

"It looks like it," Kevin said. "That's the trouble."

Jack agreed. "It underlines the weak position of women. They're exploited as much as gays are."

"Balls," Luke answered. "I mean I don't think you're wrong equating women and gays, but balls about me exploiting either."

"But you are," Kevin insisted. "You are! Like most men you've no idea that you're doing so, but that doesn't alter the fact of it."

Cheryl, however, enjoyed sharing the house and its chores with Luke. He'd always been a much more domesticated man than Aaron, and he took his turn, also, in seeing to Rebecca at night. It will be a miracle, she thought, if the child doesn't grow up a screaming neurotic, considering this peculiar first year of her life. It was surprising there were no neurotic symptoms already. But the whole situation, she decided, should end, and end soon. She could not become dependent on Luke, and Rebecca must not be deceived into thinking he was some kind of substitute father. When Aaron returned she would try and make a fresh start. She could cope now. He hadn't been in touch, not once, since he had gone to America; would *he* want to try again? If it didn't work out she would force herself to face life alone, think of herself and Rebecca as a one-parent family. The letter he had left for her she refused to take seriously. Its chief purpose, she guessed, was to jolt her into sitting up and thinking straight. She sent him a cable: "I'm back in Greenwich. Please come home."

John sat in the cottage at Roadwater, staring out of the window with unseeing eyes, or wasting the hours playing solitaire. Occasionally he wrote poems.

Almost every relationship, he told himself, had elements of sadism and masochism; one in every couple was the taker, the user, feeding on the giver, the used. So, when the taker had stolen everything there was to take, love became contempt. The user moved on, as a bee to the next flower. The winner takes it all. And thinking of the song : but tell me does she kiss like I used to kiss you? It would have been better if he had never met Luke. It had all been a waste of time, a waste of feeling. There were so few good

132

memories. He was better off as he had been, a solitary, not from choice but from bitter experience : absorbed in his work or seeking out the company of congenial friends. For sex, a pick-up in the Coleherne or a quick suck or fuck on Hampstead Heath, and if anyone stayed all night, a firm goodbye after breakfast. It was a perfectly satisfactory way of life, and so said thousands of others.

He couldn't work. It had never happened before; never, since art school, had his hands been idle. It was a living death. There was no point in trying to tell Luke, who might, perhaps, feel some guilt or pity; but what was the use of guilt or pity? It wouldn't make his hands come to life again.

Perhaps it was temporary, like love. Or was Luke, as he had feared, destroying him? The winner takes it all.

The most important experience in Luke's life, the most far-reaching in its consequences, had been the death of his father. Luke, when he first saw John, imagined him a boy, but found, instead, something of a father; or so John thought. "He's been like a curse on your whole life!" he had said on one occasion. Luke wouldn't grow up until he had exorcised that ghost. And if he could not exorcise it, he'd go on and on hurting people. On and on and on. So many kids nowadays, so many of them, pursuing what they thought was self-fulfilment – a desirable goal, society said; be yourself : do your own thing – caused only suffering, to themselves and others. "I had to come to London (or leave my lover, or break totally with my parents) in order to find myself." Crap, crap, crap! All they found was guilt; all they had to give was pain.

But he was only guessing. He knew nothing of what went on at the depths of Luke's interior, what made him function. Did anyone, he asked himself, know that of any other human being? You could only justify yourself or explain your own misery by over-emphasising your lover's weaknesses. Everybody did that, re-wrote history, re-wrote their partner's characters to suit their own needs. Nothing lasts. The wheel turns. I should try not to mourn, he said, just accept that everything is finite. Never seek the static : rejoice in the flux.

He looked again at the poem he had written yesterday. Solitaire, he'd called it.

Too tired to go to bed and too awake
To sleep, I waste the hours playing solitaire :

133

If the one lone marble is left
In the centre hole, it means tomorrow
I'll find a man, another lover.
Maybe it works.

Lover, the board like you deceives. I've asked
It once or twice, will you and I again
Be lovers? It then turns honest;
Three marbles enigmatically stare
Into the centre, saying : almost,
Almost : but no.

Solitary in this silent house. I bought
A new chair; no one sits in it except
The cat. No need to ask the board
The ultimate question, what shall I do
With myself? For I have my marbles;
I know what's what.

You too play solitaire; have played it all
Your life, played me like a fish, in games of
Loving, wee houses – two to be
Exact. The dolls' house door you slam better
Than Nora. Now you're trying solo
The game is up.

Not bad, he said to himself; then tore it into several pieces which he
threw in the wastepaper basket.

"Myrrh is mine; its bitter perfume breathes a life of gathering
gloom –"

"I've found a grey hair." Kevin was looking at himself in the
mirror.

"Sorrowing, sighing, bleeding , dying, sealed in a stone cold
tomb."

"Precisely. Grey hairs. Age. Death."

"Is the tomb stone cold in the sense of cold as a stone? Or is it a
stone tomb that also happens to be cold?" Jack lay on the sofa,
drinking coffee.

"I wasn't there."

"Myrrh. Mermaid. Myrrhmaid. Why are certain words so
attractive, like Kyle of Tongue, or Mull of Oa?" He put his mug on

the floor and stood up. "Ord of Caithness."

"How about all the Exes? Exeter, Exmouth, Exton, Exford, Exminster, Exebridge and Exwick."

"Not a fruitful line of enquiry. Besides, you forgot Up Exe and Nether Exe. Haystack."

"Rick." Kevin pulled the hair out and looked at it.

"Stack. Estuary."

"Ah. The estuary." He returned to examining his face in the mirror. There did not seem to be any other signs of the ageing process, but, he thought, that is not a boy's face; it's a man's. Something to do with the faint hints of lines at the corners of the eyes or scarring the cheeks, and the dark shadow that shaving left: how many years now of shaving; seven, eight? Nine? He couldn't remember. "Twenty-five years. A quarter of a century. A jubilee."

"Another attractive word." Jack stood behind him, also looking into the mirror. "What are you on about?"

"Age." He doesn't look any older than the day I met him, Kevin thought with some alarm. The bar in Cornwall House, Exeter University. Is that seat vacant? Yes, yes; help yourself. Was hair longer then than now? Probably. His own was an unruly mess of curls, not ginger, not copper, not brown, not black, but some half-way house. Or it was until today, until the grey thread showed itself. How many more lurked in that forest? Or in the undergrowth. Grey pubes. There were no chest hairs to worry about, and his slim slight body would always be boyish. I'm glad I'm not a man, he remembered saying once in some argument about sexism, not a *man* in that hearty he-man bath-mat-chested way Luke thinks he is, but me, male certainly and gladly, just plain old me. Luke had recently grown a beard, the long flowing Karl Marx variety. At sixteen Kevin had thought it would be easier to be a woman: just a rationalisation of a temporary unhappiness. A sex-change: what a bore, filling in all the necessary forms! Denial of self, of Kevin. Wearing women's clothes was an idea that was repellent.

"You've little to worry about," Jack said. "I'm going bald."

"You're not."

"I am. It's receding." He ran his fingers through it. "See?"

"It's the fate of blonds. Will it fall out elsewhere?" Jack's chest was curly; Kevin found this particularly attractive.

"Idiot."

Kevin gazed at him in the mirror. "Your taste in clothes never changes. You have a predilection for white. Oh, just a predilection."

"And you also wear the same old things when we go out. Leather jacket, jeans, tee-shirt. Blue or green tee-shirts."

"But I'm exceptionally subtle with the colour of my knickers. And you, you're all white. Open-necked cheesecloth and white trousers. Six pieces of clothing in search of a lost virginity."

"Lost before you met me."

"I daresay."

"I wear white because I thought it pleased you."

Kevin smiled. "It does. That rugged test cricketer, Jack Crawley, is now opening the batting for England."

"Do you fancy cricketers, then?"

"No. When you wear white, other men look at you lasciviously, especially when we're dancing. I like that."

"Why?"

"I don't know. It gives me a kick. Makes me feel I've made a pretty good choice."

"What choice? You didn't select me from a dozen others, like finding the juiciest orange in a pile at the greengrocer's."

"True. Our eyes met across a crowded room. Or some such shit."

" 'Is this seat taken?' you asked. It was, as a matter of fact."

"But you thought I looked gorgeous, sexy, and interesting."

"Something of that sort."

"And in no time at all you were wondering if I was gay too, and if I was, how soon could you get me into bed."

"*Wondering* if you were! It was obvious! I couldn't tell if *you* knew you were."

Kevin laughed. "No problem there. But we took an unconscionable time getting round to the bed part of it, didn't we? I'm glad of that. We got to know each other first. I was totally in love with you, and going half-demented because I didn't think you were with me."

"Unusual."

"What?"

"The time-lag. But when it happened, your room in Lafrowda . . . you, the first sight of you unclothed . . . I'd never dreamed someone so beautiful existed."

"I'd dreamed it all right. And there you were."

"Clumsy, apologetic, premature, the first time. But quite *superb*."

"Talking of dancing –"

"Were we?"

"A while back. It's Saturday night, which is no time for self-analysis and reminiscence. Let's go out."

"To a club?"

"Please. Torquay, where we first danced."

"Yes! What were the songs?"

" 'Seasons in the Sun'. 'Close to You'. 'Rock Your Baby'. Aaron's 'Like Us'."

"All later. Or earlier."

"Let's hit the road, baby."

They were staying with Jack's mother. She had gone to a bridge party, and wouldn't be home, she said, till one a.m.; it was an engagement she had forgotten when she invited them down. They might as well make the most of it, she added, and go out too, unless they wanted to join a lot of old ladies playing cards. Had it really slipped her mind, Jack wondered; the weekend had passed off so well that he could almost credit her with organising it deliberately as a sort of treat or reward. She had changed. To him, to both of them, though not to the dreaded subject. Which wasn't mentioned with Kevin there, but, during a few moments when he was out of the room, Jack tried to start a conversation. It was far too embarrassing. She didn't want to discuss it, ever, she said; the past was the past and she'd lived to regret her intransigence, but her attitude had not changed to *it* even if it had to *him*. As for his father, he had not budged an inch and she would not dare tell him that they had both been down to stay.

"It's a case of loving the sinner, but not the sin," Jack suggested.

"Maybe."

"The Mary Whitehouse attitude."

"I don't despise that woman. She does a good job."

"Hmm."

The most extraordinary part of it, the real measure of the compromise she had made herself accept, was that she had put them both in the same bedroom. What more could they ask, he said to Kevin. He felt enormously grateful; it released a flow of warmth and happiness in him to which Kevin responded, and

137

which quickly drew in his mother as well. Friday evening and all day Saturday were a peculiarly rich and worthwhile time as they caught up on the news and experiences of five missing years, and though Mrs Crawley never quite lost a certain anxious or nervous quality in her manner and speech, there was a smile in her eyes as they talked, in the house, or driving over the moor that morning, at lunch in the pub at Two Bridges, or when they were exploring the ruins of Okehampton Castle late in the afternoon. Kevin and he seemed to be totally as one, the inextricably combined parts of a single operation; no anecdote that was related was a soliloquy for either of them, but was told as a piece of dialogue, and any opinion he ventured was reinforced by Kevin, or something that was amusing struck them both in the same way at the same time. It was exactly the right impression to give, but it was not deliberate; it was a spontaneous thing that derived from the gift Mrs Crawley had offered them.

When they left on Sunday evening she said, "I've no need to tell you how much I've enjoyed it."

Jack, smiling up at her from behind the steering wheel of the car, said, "We have too. Very much. Both of us."

"See you soon." She bent down and kissed him, then leaned into the car and kissed Kevin as well.

When they were driving up the hill on the Exeter road, Kevin said, "Why? Why now?"

"I don't know. And it will have to remain a mystery, because she won't discuss it. Now for Dad, perhaps."

Kevin laughed. "You do push your luck!"

"I'm not under-estimating the problem."

"If she tells him we've been down, that we've slept in the same room together, in his house . . ."

"She won't say anything."

"He's a man full of hate."

"No. That's too strong."

"Is it?"

"I suppose he's very unsure of status. I think that's what it is. I'm some kind of threat to everything he wants to show the world. He's terrified of . . . being engulfed. Losing face, losing territory."

"He's lost a son."

"He doesn't see it like that. I remind him of failure. If he'd been our generation . . ."

"That's not a panacea. Not the cure for every middle-aged hang-up."

Jack tried to picture himself at fifty: pot-bellied and bald, in clothes too young for his age, a chicken-fancier, looking grotesque at discos. He'd always been attracted to the slim kind of boy, the waif-like teenager who seemed to need protection. Kevin sometimes looked so vulnerable the only answer was to smother him with kisses. In twenty years' time would Kevin still be with him? It was impossible even to guess.

Aaron, in California, felt that he had been searching all his life without realising it for somewhere completely congenial and that he had at last found it. When he thought of himself in England, of the house in Greenwich, of Cheryl, he could hardly recognise the limited, unfulfilled person he had been. His happiness did not come from anything that might previously have brought satisfaction; Aaron's Rod, for instance, on a triumphant coast-to-coast tour. He was earning enough money to live very comfortably and not draw on his English bank account; engagements were affairs of medium size and fuss, not besieged by fans nor noticed greatly by the musical press, in clubs where the crowd danced and enjoyed his singing, the playing of the group, and that was that. But it was sufficient: he no longer wanted fame, adulation, position.

It was something to do with being rootless in a society where everybody else was equally rootless, a country with not much visible history, where the past in people had often been abandoned in places across the other side of an ocean, where the future was something that mattered little, or was only a question of the next day, and the next day could probably take care of itself. Of course he was lucky; he had money and he was white. The brief glimpses he had of that other poverty-stricken Chicano society, simmering with violence, were easily shut out. Yet it existed side by side with the eternal party he lived in, almost amicably, he thought, for they seemed to feed off each other. The land was so huge: it could accommodate everything, everyone. An eternal party: swimming-pools, girls, the sea, beach barbecues, a certain quantity of drugs and alcohol that pushed it into a never-ending high, and sexual encounters that were easy and frequent, tributes to the beauty of youthful bodies and a culture of shared enthusiasms:

rock music, clothes, studied cool casualness, belief in the here and now.

Surfing became his favourite pastime. His brother Martin was an expert; Aaron had learned from him the elementary techniques on holidays at Newquay, but he had never pursued the sport with the same dedication, perhaps because he feared he would always be inferior in skill. Besides, in England there was always the endless time hanging around waiting for a wave in temperatures that were usually unpleasant, on beaches where surfers were never supreme however many of them there were, where families owned the territory by some kind of unstated divine right and regarded the malibu as an intruder, a curious and interesting object perhaps, but essentially a nuisance that disturbed the placid rhythms of seaside holidays. Here the surfer ruled; the weather was glorious, and the sea treated one kindly with wave after wave. The lack of strength in his right leg was an impediment at times, occasionally made him lose his balance and topple into the sea when the board was otherwise under his control, but it happened only when he was tired, or for some reason not absolutely relaxed. The pleasure of it, he thought, was superb, second only to sex: both were a matter of timing, unhurried cool concentration, being impelled by vast forces and ultimately succumbing to them, arriving.

He decided to stay indefinitely. He would not return, even to wind things up; Cheryl could see to that. He would not make difficulties, not oppose a divorce; he would pay for it all, settle on her whatever she required that was in his ability to give. She could have both houses. He didn't need them. He rented a small uncluttered apartment here, in Santa Monica; all he wanted from his English money was enough to buy a decent car. Then her cable arrived. He frowned, stabbed by conscience: maybe it would be better to go back, briefly, and sort it out. Seeing again the unwholesome mess of his life there could only harden his resolution to leave for good. How could he ever have thought wife and child, decades of domesticity ahead, were for him? No pressure, it was true, had been brought to bear on him to marry, to follow conventional patterns; no direct pressures that is, apart from the easily recognised and therefore easily rejected wishes of his mother to people the earth with the fruits of her sons' seed. But, as with everybody, the indirect unrecognised forces were difficult to resist. It was the done thing, the norm to which all men and women were supposed to aspire, the very foundation and fabric of society; without wife and child – that visible sign of virility – one was an outsider, regarded with pity or suspicion, gay perhaps, or thought of as having abandoned the customary procedures for selfish or eccentric reasons, a danger to wives, a hedonist preferring pleasure to responsibility, living proof of the powers that undermine society.

Even in the amoral and tolerant circles in which he had lived in England marriage was still the ultimate reason for many manoeuvres: here, in this lotus-eating paradise, it was not. The extent and influence of the gay community was one witness to this fact; he imagined, with some amusement, how Jack and Kevin would unthinkingly embrace its delights, then exclaim in horror as the foundations of their kind of marriage crumbled like a sandcastle.

"What do you *really* want?" The questioner was Jody, a gorgeous long-legged girl with peach-coloured skin. He had told her something of the situation.

"Nothing," he answered, irritated by her desire to know. He was simply enjoying lying on a beach, watching the sunset.

"But are you happy?" she persisted.

"What is it to you?"

"One's naturally curious about people."

"Why?"

She seemed unable to answer that. "One just is," she said eventually.

"I'm not."

"I don't think you'd make me happy."

"Oh I would," he said, grinning.

"There's more to it than *that.*"

"Why do you have to make everything so complicated?" He sighed, and turned away. A moment later she stood up and walked off to join a crowd of friends further along the beach. He watched her, a bit regretful: he'd hoped to spend the night with her. But it didn't really matter one way or the other.

Kevin sat in a Chelsea pub, lingering over a beer. There was no particular hurry; Jack was playing squash and wouldn't be home till ten thirty or eleven. Ray had had no illusions either about what it might lead to; he was too much involved with his dancer. This tactile exploration of a person, the discovery of mind and feelings through touch, had been quite unlike making love with Jack, whose every movement, every inch of skin, was already known. A sense of completeness: would there be a second time? Almost certainly.

There would be no post mortem with Jack. If only he had been sensible, like this, two summers ago when he returned from France, there would have been none of that awful time afterwards. What stupidity, what an expense of spirit in a waste of shame! The only risk to his life with Jack would be the desire to end it. That would never happen.

Chapter Ten

"Where is he now?" Luke asked.

"At the cottage. Why?"

"Because I think I shall go straight down there and give him a piece of my mind."

Cheryl sighed. "Don't be such an infant, Luke! What good would it do? You might end up in court."

"Don't joke about *that*."

"He knows nothing. It wouldn't matter if he did, I suppose; he's not vindictive."

"I'm going down there."

"Why?"

"Someone ought to point out that he's not behaved very well. To put it mildly."

"Big Luke."

"Big Luke. So what?"

"There's no need to shout."

He was silent for a moment, then said, "Do you want to speak to John?"

"Please."

John suggested Cheryl came to Somerset for a few days. Not at the moment, she said; there was too much chaos and confusion. Luke, upset by what she had told him and by her evident state of agitation, went out into the garden; he'd been trimming the hedge with a sickle when the phone rang. He slashed at the twigs, trying to work off his temper. Aaron had returned from California only to announce that he planned to go back there for good. Cheryl could divorce him if she wanted. She could have both the houses and most of his money. She didn't want anything from him, she'd said; she wasn't going to be the instrument to salve his guilty conscience. It was not a question of a guilty conscience, Aaron had answered coldly, just common sense. The worst of it was she'd begun to look forward to his homecoming, had thought it might all straighten out now; she was better, cured of whatever it was that had depressed her so much after Rebecca's birth. And he . . . distant and unaffectionate; he would not even kiss her, let alone stay at Greenwich, just talked of solicitors and bank managers, drawing up documents. Then he'd left, gone to the estuary to take what he wanted from the cottage. He'd not even looked into Rebecca's room – the child was asleep – not once looked at his own little daughter. She broke down and wept.

John came out into the garden. "I think I ought to go up to London with you tomorrow," he said. They had decided, at last, to break with each other : the feeling was almost like relief. They could now, on a certain level, talk amicably. John had business in London : he wanted to return to his own pottery; he had given the present occupant notice to quit. "I know Jack and Kevin are there, but they can't be expected to cope with everything. We can walk Rebecca on the heath, go shopping for her."

"Yes. If you wish." Luke put the sickle down and wiped the sweat from his face. "Listen . . . I'm going out."

"To the estuary." He nodded. "You're a fool. What's the point?"

"It will relieve my feelings."

"Grow up! A couple of kids fighting!"

"Why should I stand by and let him trample over Cheryl's life? He's got away with too much!"

"Are you sure that's why you're going?"

"What do you mean?"

"Perhaps you'll find out when you get there."

It was nearly dark when he arrived, but there was a light in the cottage. He had been wondering what he would do if Ron was out: sit and wait, he'd decided, and if his anger simmered down, just drive meekly home. But he was in. Luke was glad; now they could finish this business once and for all.

Aaron, relaxed and pleasantly surprised, offered him a drink. Luke accepted, feeling rather foolish. How did one go about this? It wasn't possible to walk into another man's house and start hitting him, call him a bastard, take that and that and that for cruelly treating an innocent and very lovely girl. "Innocent and very lovely girl": it sounded stupid and melodramatic, women's magazine stuff. Why did he want to hit him anyway? If it wasn't Cheryl who was involved, he wouldn't be bothered at all.

"You look flustered," Aaron said, sipping his gin. "What are you doing here anyway?"

"Just passing."

"Don't give me that. Did Cheryl send you?"

"No."

"What then?"

"Nothing. Nothing."

"The only reason I can think of is you want to do me over. Is that it?"

"Something like that."

Aaron laughed. "Strutting cock protecting his hen." Luke flushed, trying not to clench his fists. "What's holding you back?" Silence. "Now that you're actually here you can't bring yourself to do something so uncivilised, I suppose."

"Do you still want to writhe about in the mud?"

"Why?"

"Come on. We'll wrestle in the mud."

He laughed again. "That's absurd. What if I refuse?"

"Then I'll make you," Luke said, standing up.

"I fight dirty. Kicks in the balls."

"So do I."

Aaron lit a cigarette and thought about it. The idea appealed to him. Luke was a much bigger man of course, but it would not be an easy pushover; he considered himself no weakling, despite his lame leg. He'd played most of the sports at school, first eleven soccer, was known for endurance, tenacity. Several years ago, but the same applied to Luke. Though squash kept Luke fit. No, perhaps it was a silly idea after all: the odds were against him. A strange coincidence: when Luke abandoned Cheryl, he'd wanted to hit him for doing so. But it had seemed too childish. Instead, he'd opted for feeling superior; Luke was an insensitive intellectual, head in the clouds, of no value in the real world. Underneath that, however, he'd always felt a certain curiosity; they'd both loved the same girl. When he was in bed with Cheryl he'd sometimes remembered Luke was here before; what was it like? What did he give her that was so particularly satisfying, not just sexually, but emotionally? In every way? Who, what, was Luke? He really did want an answer to that last question. It had niggled away in his subconscious for a long time, and now, here it was, out in the open, demanding an answer. Perhaps Luke felt the same. He *must* feel the same! That was why he was here.

"Our clothes will be filthy."

"Take them off. It's nearly dark. No one's about; no one will see."

"The tide may be in."

"It isn't."

Aaron stubbed out his cigarette. "Ok," he said.

The mud was cold and so slippery it was difficult to stand, let alone walk. Some way out, when it was more than ankle deep, they stopped. It was a beautiful summer evening, not a hint of wind. The sun had set long ago, but Exmouth, facing west, was still just visible. The last of the light glinted on its panes of glass. Out at sea, the division between water and sky was barely perceptible, a faint blush which promised another day of heat. Sounds, distant and indistinguishable one from another, came from the land on both sides of the estuary, but where the two of them were standing only one noise was clear, the ooze and hiss of mud, muttering, it seemed, of its own turgid, secretive life which had been disturbed by the plop and slop of their feet. The extent of it was vast, grey and glistening in all directions, never flat but always slightly undulating, furrowed and channelled like a map of Mars.

A gull, standing on one leg, stared at them in astonishment, as if it had never before seen anything so idiotic as two humans slithering gracelessly in dark slime. It did not even think them dangerous, for it made no move to fly away. This is ridiculous, Aaron thought. "Ridiculous!" he repeated, aloud. "Shall we go indoors?"

"No."

"Then . . . how do we begin?"

"I don't know."

They stared at each other for some moments. The light had now almost totally gone; they were just outlines. Aaron shivered. He suddenly hurled himself forward, and Luke, taken by surprise, fell on his back. He sank so much that, struggling free, he left an imprint, a matrix of his body that stayed a brief moment before the mud spread out and obliterated it. He had no time to get to his feet before Aaron was on him, thrusting him down. He heaved with all his strength, pushed Aaron aside, submerged him completely. It was in his hair, his ears, his mouth. Luke allowed him to recover, watching while he kneeled in it, choking, wiping his eyes. He's serious, Aaron thought. He stood up. Undoubtedly he was the more agile of the two. He tripped Luke, pushed him underneath. It was Luke's turn to gasp and splutter. The pair of them looked identical, two floundering grey creatures exactly alike all over.

Now they were really fighting, locked together, their arms and thighs striving to grip. As they wrestled with hand or leg or hair they learned size and thickness of limb, the feeling inside the other. This gave the essence of him to Cheryl, this is what it was, his prick. He let go when Luke cried out in pain, though he wanted to twist even harder, pull it right off, but Luke was now on top of him, spread-eagled, triumphant, turning him over, hands under him, lifting him out of the mud, slowly but irresistibly up, over his shoulder like a sack of coal, then throwing him away, splat! And the mud hit him, winding him, swallowing him up. He lay in it, quite still.

"Enough?" Luke panted, and in reply, Aaron grabbed at his knees, crashing him down. But he was quickly back to his feet. He pulled Aaron closer, legs round his legs, arms pinioning him in a hold so tight that Ron's face was crushed against his chest. They slipped and toppled over. Aaron sank, cracking his head on a stone. He was fighting for breath for the slime was in his nose and mouth again. "Do you give in?" Luke cried, but Ron, spitting out mud, could not answer. Luke dragged him up, shouting "Give in, you fool!" then forced him under a second time. Weaker, and feeling frightened, he was relieved when Luke unexpectedly let him go, turned, and started to wade back towards the shore. He called out, "Wait for me!" He was shaking, exhausted, only just able to walk. He wiped the mud from one hand with the other, then smeared it away from his mouth. Luke stopped till he caught up, put an arm round his shoulder, and together they trudged back to the cottage.

"A bath, I think," Aaron said.

"It would help."

"We can shower or bath."

"Shower."

It was small, meant only for one, but they both stood under it, the hot water slowly peeling off the mud, transforming them into recognisable pink human beings. They washed each other's hair. As the dirt slipped away they discovered they were bleeding, Ron from a cut on the back of his head, Luke from a grazed elbow and swollen lip, both of them in several places on their feet. "Like Psycho," Ron said, as he watched blood mingle with water and swirl down the plug-hole. "I've some elastoplast somewhere."

"I'm whacked!" Luke slid down the wall of the shower into a sitting position. Aaron did the same. Their legs touched. Luke smiled. "I enjoyed it," he said. "I don't know why, but I did."

"Me too. Even though I lost."

"I wasn't thinking of it like that. It was a kind of . . . meeting-ground."

Aaron nodded, agreeing. "We ought to go out and find a girl. With big knockers."

"To share? Three in a bed?"

"Yes."

"We already have. In a sense."

"I'm impressed by what she found."

"So am I."

They both grinned, as if it was a conspiracy between two small boys. "I seem to be erect," Aaron said.

"So I observe . . . Do you . . . want to do something about it?"

"If . . . you like."

Another conspiracy between two boys : tossing each other off.

"I'd like to screw you," Luke said.

"No way! Even this . . . I haven't done this since I was fourteen." Not just a minute of lust : they kissed; their hands explored skin; they embraced with their whole bodies. Suddenly, it was almost passionate as they allowed each other to see their desire to know. Both cocks in Luke's right hand; deliberately he delayed orgasm, delayed it again, a third, a fourth time, enjoying Aaron's harsh breathing, the sounds of his pleasure, watching his eyes, seeing what Cheryl had seen. More than physical sensation: what was it? How could he define it? Self-ness. Yes. As Aaron, similarly, was experiencing his. "I can't hold back any longer!" Ron cried out.

Minutes later Luke opened his hand, smearing it on both their skins as if he was sharing equally a gift each had given the other.

"The mud-fight was a way of saying we wanted to do that," Luke said.

"I know."

"John's favourite song of the moment: 'But Tell Me Does She Kiss Like I Used to Kiss You?' "

"Yes. But more than that. Wasn't it?"

"Yes."

They sat in the lounge, in silence, sharing a joint. After a while Luke asked, "What's the time?"

"Nearly midnight."

"I like the idea of us sharing a girl."

"One day we will."

He yawned. "I must go home."

"You can stay if you want to."

"I feel bloody tired." He stretched out on the sofa, and almost immediately he was asleep. Aaron fetched the quilt from the spare room and covered him with it.

Some hours later Luke woke, dressed hurriedly, and left. He was weary in every bone and muscle. It was half past five in the morning. Already the estuary was busy with a life which would be much less apparent in full daylight, muted when people were present. Now it belonged to the birds, great crowds of them winging across the water, chattering, calling to each other. Gulls squawked and squabbled over a fish. Mallards quacked. Two Canada geese. Plovers. Kingfishers, a fulmar, the S shape of a cormorant. The tide was in, lapping the walls. Reeds rustled. Last night's battleground had vanished; it was impossible even to guess where it had been.

He drove home, watching the sun rise. He had not often seen a summer dawn. As he approached Exeter, the twin towers of the cathedral were gold in the morning. The city slept. The valley through Bickleigh, Tiverton, Bampton was astonishingly beautiful, like the beginning of the world. Two milkmen in Tiverton and a man standing on Bickleigh Bridge were the only people he saw. Up now on the top of the land, the edges of Exmoor, the Watchet road, great panoramas of wild hill-country. He stopped at the summit of the incline and looked down at the dark trees below, the distant sea. Fields, hills. A marvellous warm day ahead, and he had to drive to London! It was a day for doing nothing, just existing in the countryside or plunging into the sea. He sniffed his hand. Despite the shower last night, he still smelled of the estuary, a complex combination of fish, salt, sea-weed, sewage. A dank, chill odour of river-mouth. And, more pleasantly, the smell of Aaron. They would probably never do it again, but he hoped they would keep in touch, write to each other.

He crept indoors and slipped into bed beside John. Over breakfast he apologised for staying out so late and presumably causing a lot of worry.

"I wasn't worried," John said. "Aaron phoned at about half past midnight. He said you were asleep."

"That was thoughtful of him."

"Maybe he learned something too."

"I daresay."

"When did he last have sex with a man?"

Luke stared at him, surprised. "Did he tell you?"

"Of course not. But it was perfectly obvious you were going to. That was why you went."

"Was it? It wasn't obvious to me. It just . . . happened; that's all. Are you jealous?"

"Naturally. Two extremely attractive men having it off together. And *I'm* the one who's gay! Superb irony!"

Luke laughed. "That's the way the cookie crumbles," he said.

"You and I . . . I guess we're well rid of each other."

"I wonder if this will be my last morning here." He gazed at the things of the room. "All that effort . . . the painting, the carpentry . . . the affection put into it . . . all wasted."

"*I* still have the benefits. Perhaps you'll become known as the man who only stops long enough to decorate his lovers' houses."

They looked at each other with intense dislike.

"They were doing *what?*" Kevin was aghast.

"Fighting in the mud," John said. Jack looked impassive, Cheryl annoyed.

"Pair of stupid bullcalves roaring over territory."

"Territory?" Luke giggled, enjoying Kevin's disapproval.

"Territory, a female, it's all the same thing. Primitive cave-man stuff, sexist male pigs shouting I'm the greatest! I'm the only big he-man there is, proving the hairs on my chest aren't false! What are you so worried about? You'd have both been far better off jumping into bed together if you really wanted contact with your own sex." Jack and Cheryl laughed, but John and Luke were so peculiarly silent that Kevin wondered for a moment if that was what had really happened. His dismissed the idea at once; it was so wildly unlikely.

They were in Cheryl's sitting-room. Rebecca was playing quietly in a corner with some building bricks. The key turned in the lock: Aaron. Everyone fell silent. "Do you mind if I talk to Cheryl alone?" he asked.

"No, no, of course not," they murmured, so Rebecca and her toys were picked up, ready to be taken away. Wheresoever the carcass is, there shall the eagles be gathered together, Luke thought. Though John, Jack, Aaron and Kevin were not exactly eagles, nor was Cheryl yet a carcass. Rebecca protested, kicking her father and thumping him with little fists; she wanted to go on playing.

"Leave her," Cheryl said.

"Are you sure?" Kevin asked.

"Yes."

Luke nodded in the direction of the kitchen door, and Aaron, taking the hint, went out there with him. "I don't know if we'll meet again, just the two of us."

"I'm in London for a week, then – "

"Yes. Well . . . I wanted to say . . . write to me."

"I will. I'd planned to do that."

"And . . . good luck. I mean it." They smiled at each other.

Later, after Aaron had left, Cheryl brought Rebecca downstairs. She had been crying. "It was all legal talk," she said. "Wills and settlements. Bloody . . . I think I shall sell the cottage. I'll need the money, and I never liked the place. Damp and poky."

"Don't do anything in a rush," Jack said. "Kevin and I might decide to buy it from you."

"What for?"

"It's just an idea. We were thinking we might move out of London if we can find jobs. It's handy there . . . Exeter, my mother. And Kevin's parents not too far up the M5. Though I don't yet know if we can find enough for a deposit."

"Well . . . all in good time. I can't think about it at the moment."

"Yes. Yes . . . I understand."

"He's gone. He's taken what he wants from the flat and gone! We shan't see him again. Ever!" She put her arms round Kevin and wept. But John pulled her gently away and led her upstairs, saying she should rest, or have something to drink, or a sedative, and not to worry about meals: he would cook, or Luke; they would stay with her, see her through the worst. Luke raised his hands in a gesture of despair. After they had gone, Jack and Kevin sat together in silence. It was too late for words.

Kevin, needing to do something, went into the kitchen and started to make a cake. A fairly complicated thing he decided, not a sponge or a madeira, but a rich, exotic creation that would demand all his attention. A Christmas cake. Why not, even if it was the first of August, the weather oppressive and sultry? He, perhaps, of Cheryl's friends was the most outraged by what Aaron had done. Bastard, he kept saying as he pummelled margarine, sugar, and flour; bastard!! Just as he himself had been, at an earlier time, with Jack. But somehow it seemed worse that it was a woman who was being maltreated, unlike, in his own case, another man: a man was expected to survive a crisis more easily. Which was evident nonsense; he'd driven Jack almost to breaking point. Though there was no baby to bring up single-handed. What would she do? She'd talked of returning to her old job at the building society, but what would happen to Rebecca if she did? Parked in some crèche or nursery all day long. It was worse for a woman, much worse, and it was wrong, all wrong, that that should be so. He'd like to see a time when women and gays joined forces to destroy the domination of heterosexual man.

Compared with Cheryl his own problems were slight, though there were a few dark clouds. Jack had received a very nasty letter from his father. Mrs Crawley, apparently, had told her husband of the trip to Okehampton, and he had not been pleased. The letter said that Jack was, of course, welcome at home whenever he wished to come, but not if he brought Kevin with him. It was time he showed a little more sense of responsibility and realised that he had duties to his parents. He owed them some gratitude for everything they had done for him, the sacrifices they had made, and the best way of going about repaying such a debt was not to fly in the face of their most deeply held wishes and beliefs. Jack, in a furious temper, tore the letter into tiny pieces. He was depressed and edgy for days afterwards.

The other difficulty concerned Chris and Ray. He had not seen Ray a second time, but he didn't know if Jack had seen Chris. It was a subject they had agreed not to mention; Kevin, in particular, had stressed that he did not want to know. Yet he did, of course.

Was it a sign that something was fundamentally wrong if he and Jack couldn't satisfy each other totally? Would their relationship drift, as he had observed with so many gay couples who had been together for years, five years, ten, fifteen, into an easy companionship, much needed certainly, and never on the point of disintegration, but one in which they always sought sexual pleasure not with each other, but outside, even hunted for it together? The idea was repellent. Of course there were periods of sexual boredom: Ray and Chris were a symptom of it, but those times were temporary. He couldn't envisage himself, for good and all, growing weary of Jack in bed; but there was always a chance Jack might grow weary of him. Jack was so bloody attractive! The honey-pot and the proverbial bees. It added anxiety to those moments when he said no, I'm too tired; and Jack wasn't. Or when Jack said no. The I've-just-washed-my-hair syndrome. He'd discussed the problem over the phone with Ray, who told him he was making mountains out of molehills. And when was he coming over again? Some time or other, Kevin said, refusing to be pushed into a definite arrangement.

"The smell is gorgeous," Jack said, coming into the kitchen. "What is it?"

"Christmas cake. And you are *not* to touch it until it's properly marzipanned and iced."

"Christmas cake!" Jack laughed. "What a sweet idea! Love – "

"Yes?"

"I do love you."

When Jack said one day that he hoped it would not be long before Cheryl found somebody else, she replied, rather angrily, that having been abandoned by two men did not mean she was in a really great rush to fly into the arms of a third. He was struck by her bitterness. Both he and Kevin began to find they needed to take care over what they talked about with her; they often discovered they were under attack when they had only intended to be well-meaning. It was largely because they were the nearest, the most available, but they were hurt when Cheryl claimed that they did not understand her, that they couldn't possibly know what she had gone through. They were not like most men, they argued; they were gay, and were therefore in a particularly good position to sympathise with the problems of women. What about women who were homosexual, Cheryl wanted to know? The women gay men liked were all straight, weren't they? How many lesbians did they number among their friends? When they used the word 'gay', weren't they thinking, for ninety-nine per cent of the time, of men? When Kevin said something about militant aggressive dykes frightening off those males who wanted to help them most, Cheryl merely said it was inevitable; what else could he expect?

Sexual politics was not an area in which Jack or Kevin were much interested, let alone informed. They did not join protest marches, or wave banners for gay liberation; they preferred the comfort and warmth of the ghetto: the club or the pub. When they read *Gay News* it was for the articles or the advertisements on the back pages, rather than finding out what a group in Luton or Leicester had achieved by lobbying an M.P. Not that they ever answered the adverts, but their eccentricity they frequently found laughable, sometimes pathetic: "Eighty-year-old seeks coloured boy, 21 plus, for long-lasting stable friendship" or "Covent Garden crush bar, October 13th. You in denim, me yellow sweater. You smiled. Please contact." Their complacency on the subject of gay rights was beginning to be shaken, however, not only from the unexpected quarter of Cheryl, but from the example of Chris and Ray, who were deeply committed to such matters. Ray cared. His photograph was often to be seen in *Gay News*.

Cheryl joined an organisation for one-parent families and began to attend meetings on women's rights, usually taking Rebecca with her. Though she had gone back to her old job, leaving the child at a nursery, she had plenty of time to brood. She had few close friends in London, and no particular hobbies to fill her time. She saw Jack and Kevin daily, either for a meal or a late-night cup of tea, but she resisted all their offers to help in other ways. She had to find strength inside herself. She'd never done so; it was high time she learned to survive alone. She had gone from one situation to another in which men had dominated her, forcing her to act out the person they felt she ought to be. It was inevitable, of course, that she should wonder what was so wrong with herself that she had twice been deserted, but meditating on that was something she began to avoid; it only led to depression and the wretched trap of non-stop self-analysis. There was nothing wrong with her. In both instances she'd been badgered by the men into starting the relationship, and it was their inadequacies that had brought it to an end.

Walking for miles wheeling Rebecca's pushchair became her favourite pastime. Greenwich, she discovered, was fascinating; she was amazed she had never realised it before. It was not only for its obvious and spectacular pieces of history – the Cutty Sark, Hawksmoor's church, Inigo Jones's palace, the observatory, Wren's naval college – that she began to love the place; the park, the views of London, and the expanse of Blackheath were also beautiful. And the little streets of terraced houses that led to the river, untouched by Nazi bombs or exploiting developers; the long frontage by the Thames, past the college and the riverside pubs into a world of warehouses, moored ships and factories. Where the river swept in a great curve round the Isle of Dogs was unvisited by people in the evening, the ships deserted, the warehouses and factories shut up for the night: smells of new timber, malt, vegetables. There was a certain weariness about it all, a patience, a melancholy, that suited her very well. If Jack and Kevin were with her they sometimes stopped for a drink at the Yacht, or, going under the river by the foot tunnel, they would explore the Isle of Dogs side, and have a beer at the Waterman's Arms or the Gun. They drank outside, sitting on the wall, gazing down into the detritus the Thames had on show that day: rotting wood and paper, the bloated corpse of a dead dog, bottles, contraceptives so enormous that they must have been filled by giants.

Loneliness was the hardest problem. Life, for better or worse, was essentially couple-orientated, and early conditioning was not usually, and definitely not in her case, an education for single adulthood. Even buying food reminded her that the world catered for pairs; it was always impossible in the supermarket, for instance, to buy just *one* pork chop. Though her day was busy (there was rarely an occasion when she said to herself, I'm bored, I've got nothing to do) there were never any high moments. Small things began to irritate her that once had been no bother; certain television personalities were particularly annoying – Larry Grayson, Jimmy Saville, O.B.E. (why insist on the inclusion of that?), Jim Davidson; but worst of all was John Noakes. Why this decent and faintly dotty person should so upset her she found hard to pin down. She watched him one afternoon when it was too wet and windy to take Rebecca out; he was climbing Nelson's Column and she kept hoping he would fall off. It was something to do with his voice, she thought (it was so loud and insistent), and the perpetual image of the overgrown schoolboy clown being dreadfully enthusiastic about matters of the utmost insignificance. Maybe it put her in touch with what she resented about Luke and Aaron, both insistent and enthusiastic men, in their opinions, their obsessions, their seduction of her. The difference in their obsessions and John Noakes's was unimportant. Rock music, classical music, English literature, squash, or climbing Nelson's Column: it didn't matter what; they were merely more elaborate versions of schoolboy crazes like collecting stamps, games to pass the time. If there should ever be another man in her life it would have to be someone totally different. She decided against divorce proceedings. It would be expensive and distressing, and not leave her any better off than she was now. If she were to marry again, that would be time enough to do so. But it was unlikely. What was the point? A ceremony, a binding contract: she needed none of that. It was simply another ball and chain.

Her mother-in-law took to ringing her up once a week. This also was exceedingly irritating. Cheryl wanted to have nothing to do with the Brown family any more; her connection with them was severed: why constantly inflame the raw nerve-ends of it? Doris had had a letter from Aaron, posted in Los Angeles, giving the bare outline of what had happened. Though very upset, she wanted detail, suggested Cheryl came to stay, and after the fourth or fifth refusal she said, pointedly, that Rebecca was *her* grandchild, her *only* grand-daughter. She was loud and effusive in her sympathy for Cheryl's present situation, but she could not make herself put all the blame on Aaron; the idea of any son of *hers* being completely in the wrong was impossible. Cheryl wished she could be so rude to Doris that she would never phone again, but she was not able to bring herself to do this. So the weekly conversation continued, and added to her melancholy.

A French teacher was wanted at the comprehensive school in Teignmouth and Jack applied, successfully. Kevin decided he had no choice but to resign his job too; he wrote off for every available teaching post in Devon, but no one required his services. In September he would be on the dole, not a prospect he was looking forward to.

156

Jack made Cheryl an offer on the cottage, but he was not sure that he was in a position to buy it : he could borrow ninety per cent of the money from a building society, but had no means of obtaining the rest, so in desperation he telephoned his mother to see if she could help. A few days later Mr Crawley sent a curt postcard: "Come down and we'll discuss it." Kevin went with him, but Jack, for the first time, set his principles aside: it would be more tactful if his lover stayed the night at the Woods' farm. Kevin needed no second bidding.

Mr Crawley asked Jack how he was. Did he like teaching, and was he still living with Kevin? He looked at his son sadly, and said, "Why don't you try to give it up?"

"Give up what?"

"This . . . homosexual thing." He paused for a moment, then said, "Take me as an example. I've smoked a pipe all my adult life. I've never tried to kick the habit, but I could if I had to. Tomorrow. Why don't you do the same with this . . . this . . . "

"They're not alike." Jack was acutely embarrassed, but at the same time he wanted to laugh at the absurd analogy.

Mr Crawley frowned. Why is it, Jack wondered, he still has the power to frighten me? We're both grown men. Yet he scares me as if I were a kid! He had the kind of face that children feared, craggy, with huge eyebrows and an unsmiling mouth. It was useful at the bank; it persuaded customers not to push too far with their overdrafts, but it had never helped in dealing with his sons. Jack remembered how much, as a child, he'd disliked the smell of his father: alcohol, tobacco.

"What is it, then? Are you scared of women; is that it? Don't think you're good enough to find one?"

"Not that at all!"

"You can't prefer a man to a woman."

"Thousands of men do."

"Rubbish." The idea was swept aside. Mr Crawley thought it impossible, so it could not exist. "My son pretending to be a woman. Or is it him? One of you, anyway."

"No one's pretending to be anything different from what they are."

"On the increase, of course. Every blessed television programme has one these days. You can't switch the damn thing on without some pansified freak flapping his wrists at you or waving a handbag. Oh, I've seen them for myself! Some pub I went to in Exeter. Never again! I was downright ashamed walking in there with your mother. A spell in the army, that would sort them out."

Jack stood up. "This is getting us nowhere," he said.

"What about the money you want to borrow?" Jack was silent. "You can have it," Mr Crawley said, enjoying the look of surprise on his son's face. "I'll write you a cheque now. You can make a banker's order for twenty pounds a month till it's paid off. Interest free. What do you say?"

"That there must be a snag."

"No, no. A condition. The cottage is in your name and your name alone. I'm not having that creature laying his hands on my money. And I want a written statement to that effect."

"Written . . .?"

"And you must make a will, of course. Most men make wills when they're buying property, and they take out an insurance policy so their wives can inherit without having to go on paying the mortgage. But you don't have a wife. So I want you to make a will, leaving the house to someone in this family, us, or your brother, or his children if he ever has any."

"I've already made a will."

"Oh?"

"All I have, which isn't much, goes to Kevin."

"You'll have to make another one, then."

"No. You can stuff your money." He went over to the door. "Goodbye, Mum." Mrs Crawley had been present during the entire conversation. She was sitting on the sofa, her back to them, only the top of her head visible. She stared into the fire, from time to time wringing her hands. Jack couldn't stop himself saying sarcastically as he left the room "Thanks for your help, Mum. It really did make a difference."

He drove up to the farm, scarcely aware of passing traffic or how dangerously near, at sharp bends, he came to crashing the car into the wall. Kevin was in the kitchen, alone. One glance at his lover told him everything. "Fucking shit," Jack muttered, close to tears.

Kevin put his arms round him. "Calm down," he said. "Calm down."

"I *hate* him! And her. She didn't say a word! I'll never go back there. Never! Never!"

158

"Ssh. Ssh. Jack! Please. It's me, love."

"Yes."

"Kiss me."

The tears came, and Kevin's face, touching Jack's, was wet and salty. "Kevin. Darling! Help me!"

"It doesn't matter about the cottage. Really it doesn't. We'll rent a flat somewhere."

"How can a man . . . how can he make his grown-up son weep? I'm not six, I'm twenty-six! I'll never forgive him. Never!" He broke away and sat down at the table, trembling violently. "He called you . . . that creature."

"Sticks and stones."

"Don't be silly. Words *do* hurt! Very much!"

"Let's go home."

"It's time we made a stand. Demand our rights! I've had enough! Being treated worse than a dog!"

"Come on." Kevin pulled him to his feet.

A few days later a cheque arrived at the flat. Pay J.M. Crawley one thousand pounds. It was in his mother's handwriting and signed by her. There was no letter, no explanation. "What the hell does it mean?" Jack asked, bewildered.

"Ring her up and ask," Kevin said, as he brushed his teeth. "And buy some toothpaste, Jack. We're nearly out. I must go; I'm late."

They had a joint account, his mother told him. She'd written him a letter, but in her hurry to send the money off, she'd forgotten to put it in the envelope. "So . . . you mean he doesn't know," Jack said. That's right; the cheque should be paid in at once before he found out and stopped it. "I don't know whether I ought to," he said, doubtfully. Nonsense. When it was done it was done; there was nothing his father could do except rant and rave.

Which he did, a week later, when he came to examine his bank statement. She was expecting the onslaught; it was only a question of when it would happen. It was tantamount to fraud and embezzlement, Mr Crawley said, thumping the dining-room table; how could she do such a thing? He sulked and shouted alternately, threatened and abused her, but there was no concrete action he could take. "I'd like to know which of my clerks let that through," he said. "I'll throttle him!" It would be advisable, she said over the phone to Jack, not to come down to Okehampton for a while. He

159

laughed. "That's the understatement of the year! But thanks, Mum. Thanks for everything."

"Is it all going through? No problems with the building society?"

"No."

There was one problem, however; the difficulties that seemed to ensue if the cottage was in their joint names led them to decide that officially Jack should be the sole owner. More discrimination, he said, certain that the building society manager had guessed they were both gay and didn't like it, thought it might be an unsafe proposition for the society's funds. Oh, yes, people like that, so unstable! Their relationships never last more than a year or two, and then who'd pay the mortgage? Kevin, however, was more philosophical, though he imagined there might perhaps be trouble if they ever did split up. He could be left homeless.

Chapter Eleven

Luke, alone now in London, got down to the business of resuming what he called his real life. It was a return to bed-sitter land, one room in a tumbledown place in Kentish Town, the area he had lived in when he had first been a student. Domestic existence was supplied happily enough by the other people in the house. The kitchen and the living-room were shared with them, all young transients like himself; so he was rarely alone at meal-times or if he chose to stay in for an evening to watch television. If he went out there were colleagues from work to drink with, parties he was invited to. And it was easy enough to find girls. Always girls now : the past few years he considered were definitely an aberration, an interesting enough experience, but one he was glad to put behind him. Sex with girls, he decided, was a lot more satisfying than sex with men. The plumbing was better, and the softness of female flesh aroused him much more than John's lean, slim body. On one occasion, a favourite fantasy of his became a reality when he bedded two at once. Never before had he felt so macho; it turned him on so much that he was able to have, for him, a record number of orgasms in one night. What more could I want out of life, he asked himself next day.

It never occurred to him, when he thought of the years with John, that he was re-writing his existence, obliterating this or embroidering that in order to make sense of the way he had behaved. As he thought of reasons for events, he forgot that he'd always told himself to play it by ear. The shape and pattern he was now imposing on his own past ignored the fact that most of his life with John had been spontaneous, was reaction to things of the moment, pleasurable or painful as the case might be. So, eventually, that past had for him a spurious intellectual structure, like the plot of a novel with a neat beginning, middle, and end, in which he was the hero – a young, exploited ingénu – and John was the villain, old and manipulative, using his experience to satisfy his selfish, kinky urges. So, a record number of orgasms with two girls he hardly knew and didn't particularly want to know except as vessels for sperm, became in his mind a vastly superior experience to the night of love-making with John that first Christmas.

Nor did he think very clearly about the future. A wife and children one day. It was bound to happen; he was sure of it. The same cheerful certainty applied to his work. He was good at his job and he loved it, though he would soon move on : there was no doubt in his mind. Our man in Mogadishu.

He was standing still, but thinking he was living. It was a virtue now, he thought, that he never wanted to say to anyone, "I love you."

He saw little of Cheryl, or Jack and Kevin. On one of the rare occasions he was at the house in Greenwich, he found a letter waiting for him. From Australia, from his brother Adam; it had been sent care of Jack because Adam had no idea of Luke's present address. The news it contained was so startling that he read it aloud to the others. After six years of marriage Adam and his wife had decided on a divorce; he proposed to return to England as soon as he could.

"I went out with him once or twice before I knew Luke," Cheryl said to Kevin.

"Did you?"

"Oh, nothing serious."

"I don't think I've ever met him."

"You have met him," Jack said. "At my brother's eighteenth-birthday party."

"I don't remember. What's he like?"

"A quieter version of Luke," Cheryl said. "Altogether less . . . what's the word? Simply less, I suppose."

Luke, reading the letter again, looked up and said, "What do you mean by that?"

"Not so tall, not so good-looking, not such dark hair, less extreme, less physical, less arrogant . . . hmmm. Dare I say it?"

"You will anyway," Luke said.

"In many respects a much nicer person."

Kevin and Jack laughed, but Luke was not amused. "I don't really care a fuck what any of you think," he said. That produced a strained silence, and he left a few moments later.

"Without realising it," Jack said, "he probably told us something quite true just now."

"What?" Cheryl asked.

"That he doesn't care a fuck what any of us think."

She sighed. "Yes."

"And if you feel that about people it means you no longer value them. No longer need them. Soon he'll be disappearing out of our lives."

"Will you be sorry?"

"Yes." He frowned. "However . . . it will be good to see Adam again."

Kevin was no nearer to sorting out the muddle of his responses to Ray and Chris. It was not fear of the catastrophe his return from France had brought; there was indeed a positive gain: a re-assertion of independence, the pleasure of someone else's interest which marvellously refreshed life with Jack, pushed more positive energies into their relationship, stopped it consisting entirely of medium-level reactions. Was that true? Wasn't it perhaps only vanity? Seeking proof that he was still physically desirable, that habit had not deadened everything, that he wasn't shut off in a cell that, however pleasant, was nevertheless a prison, a gilded cage? All of these things, probably, and, if it was merely an indication of the more selfish instincts, it was necessary in order that the loving giving part of his nature should function properly. That didn't sound moral, he decided, then he would say to himself, whose morality? His own, or some vaguer, more general kind of ethic which most people aspired to in an unthinking kind of way, and occasionally, when the rational processes were at their keenest, sharply rejected? At this point he usually stopped trying to work it out. Inevitably perhaps, he had been with Ray a second time, a third, a fourth.

For such behaviour not to damage his life with Jack necessitated a much higher degree of awareness of his lover's feelings, a finer attention to points of detail than he was sometimes capable of, and the same was equally true for Jack, who had continued to see

Chris. It was as if they had both tired of steering a ship in an untroubled pond and had mutually agreed to push it through choppier waters, but the steering required skills that could only be learned rather painfully. They wanted the sharpening of senses that risk and danger produced, yet when they were out together they needed each other's absolute attention. Jack, dancing with Kevin on one occasion, was anywhere else than with his partner, staring at other people, his feet shuffling to the music: Kevin's anger was such that his good temper was not restored for hours, so late that the evening was ruined. Once upon a time, when they had chained themselves together with demands of total fidelity, it would not have mattered: they would both probably have been shuffling to the music and looking at the door, wondering who was coming in next.

Jack read the message correctly and it did not happen again. A particular kind of closeness began to develop between them that was at its most obvious when they were with a gay crowd, not the kind of total exclusiveness lovers in their first month of an affair seemed to exude, but a feeling that the one was not complete without the other's presence: in a pub they had, in the past, not necessarily spent their time cheek by jowl, but talked to friends, saying it wasn't necessary, being together for the rest of the day or night, to monopolise each other. Now they became almost a double act; a story told, or a joke, was as if they were one person with two bodies.

"Nothing is static with us," Kevin said one evening. "I keep feeling there's a whole lot more inside us to unlock."

"This flat's static," Jack answered, looking round at the walls of the kitchen. "It hasn't been painted for years."

"We have a house now. I'm looking forward to that . . . I think."

"So am I. Very much."

There will be less going out in the evenings, Jack thought; the cottage is remote : every journey will be an effort. Five or six miles by car to Exeter, to a film or the theatre, a concert or the gay pub, on top of five or six miles each day to work. They simply wouldn't want to be away from home as often as they were now. Their own house: no Cheryl upstairs; she was so much a part of their daily lives, particularly Kevin's. Furnishing and decorating, watching things grow in their garden, absorbing the estuary: the two of them alone. The silence of the country at night. Such a different structure to the pattern of their lives might produce a whole new set of strains and stresses. Were they ready for this? Yes, they probably were. He relied once more on what was always his ultimate measure of judgement: the absence of Kevin was a kind of death, his presence the only thing that made life in any way worthwhile.

These thoughts were still in his head when Chris found him at the squash club that evening, were still there later when he was holding the boy in his arms. Chris the waif, the thin puny body all bones and odd angles, needing protection; why did he respond, when Kevin, too, had that appeal, and so much more? Perhaps because it was only one small aspect of Kevin, concealing an interior toughness of mind. Chris really was a waif: he could let Jack play out some fantasy he needed to fulfil, the uncle, the casual provider of sweets, just as Kevin found in Ray's campaigning, his foreignness, his air of knowing the answers, something Jack could not give him.

"I shan't see you again," he said to Chris.

The kid looked lost and hurt. "Why?"

"The other two. That's why."

"Nonsense."

"I mean it. I shan't see you again."

"Maybe."

They'd had this conversation before.

In August, Jack and Kevin moved to the cottage on the estuary. To celebrate, Kevin suggested, why not ask Cheryl to come down for a day or two? And John, who was at the house in Somerset; Luke too – Luke was also in Somerset. He had had to return to Minehead : the hospital had written to him at last with a date for the removal of the warts and the cyst.

"Mad," Jack said. "Where do we put them all? Including us there are five adults and one child. We have precisely two bedrooms."

"Cheryl can have the single bed, and we'll ask her to bring a mattress for Rebecca. John can sleep on the sofa."

"Teeming humanity. Where are you going to put Luke?"

"He and John can sort something out."

"Are they on speaking terms these days?"

"Must be, as Luke is staying at Roadwater."

"Hmmm."

165

But there was a sixth adult, a quite unexpected guest : Luke's brother. He had returned from Australia in April, and found himself a job with a firm in London. He came over to Greenwich on several occasions. Jack and he had been in the same form at school, and though later it was Luke who had become the close friend, it didn't seem odd that Adam should seek out Jack when he returned alone and friendless, trying to make a new life in a city that must at first have struck him as quite foreign after an absence from England of six years. Jack could see in him how the passage of time marked people in a way he could not assess with himself or with Kevin: the lines on the face, the fat under the chin, the hairline receding a little. It was a bit horrifying: he must present a similar picture himself. "No, no," Adam reassured him. "We're grown-up now, that's all. I know we thought we were at twenty, but we weren't." It was strange, the slight Australian accent; it took some getting used to.

It was not Jack that Adam came to see on his third or fourth, or subsequent, visits to Greenwich; it was Cheryl. There seemed nothing in it: both were so understandably wary and tentative after a smashed-up marriage. But one Saturday morning Kevin met him in the hall picking up the milk. He hurried back inside and woke Jack with the news : "He stayed the night!!"

"Who? What are you talking about?"

"Adam!"

"Where?"

"With Cheryl, of course!"

"Oh." Jack turned over and went to sleep again.

It appeared to the observers downstairs, however, to be something less than instant infatuation. Adam didn't move in; he just stayed overnight from time to time. Cheryl didn't discuss it with Kevin. So it was a considerable surprise when he turned up at the cottage with her, driving her car. Luke, who knew no more than Jack and Kevin did, was equally startled.

Luke said that he could only stop one night; he had to return to Minehead in the morning to go into hospital. "What is this operation?" Cheryl asked.

Luke explained, and Jack shuddered. "I'd hate the idea of a knife in that part of my body!" he said.

"Nobody's going to use a knife! I hope. I think they burn them out."

"Maybe they'll cut his balls off while they're at it," John said.

In the evening they wanted to walk to the Turf, but who should remain behind to look after Rebecca? Not me, Cheryl protested : she was housebound most days of the year; nor Kevin: he had cooked for them all and deserved a break. Nor me, Luke said. He was in danger of losing his raison d'être on the morrow; the condemned man's last request. Adam agreed to stay, and Jack decided to keep him company. The Turf was crowded with boating people. Kevin, holding Cheryl's hand, said, "They probably think you and I are lovers having a Friday night out."

Cheryl laughed. "If only they knew the truth!"

"I'll tell them. I'll wear my badge."

"What badge?"

He took it out of his jeans pocket and pinned it to his tee-shirt. GLAD TO BE GAY it shrieked.

"Where on *earth* did you get that?"

"Ray."

Luke read it aloud, and said, "Why?"

"Why not?" Kevin asked.

"People don't go around proclaiming they're glad to be straight, do they? They just are."

"Well . . . maybe the wording is a bit wrong."

"Oh, Kevin! You'd be useless on the barricades!"

"What do you mean?"

"At the first shot you fall off. Learn some verbal self-defence!"

At least, in the coming months, if there was nothing else to do, he could learn how to read the beauty of the estuary, Kevin thought. The tide was half-way out as they walked home. A bird with a long curved beak flew overhead, a snipe, or was it a curlew? A cormorant dived, stayed under the water for so long that it seemed impossible it should not drown: it surfaced, yards away, smoothing its feathers, its head a little to one side as if inviting admiration from the humans watching on the sea-wall.

A heron flapped by, slow and dignified. "Dragging its slow length along," Luke said.

The course of the river between the mud-flats was a mystery; why did it move in a series of coils like a giant serpent, instead of pushing its way straight through the silt? Mooring buoys marked its progress, and forlorn structures of bleached wood like blasted trees. The sun, below the hills to their right, flamed the woods on

167

the ridge. Thin lines of cloud – red, green, and purple, all sunset colours – streaked the sky. A pair of swans flew between two of the lines, wings creaking. Where the estuary joined the sea was Exmouth, a glittering flimsy web of light, only its church tower solid. Perhaps they should go there by boat, Kevin thought; there had always been this view of it, but further down a whole new set of vistas would be opened up, some kind of explanation, he imagined, of the landscape, of how river joined sea, of what Exmouth was doing there, huddled into that last corner of land, and why this great gash in the structure of Devon with its teeming bird-life, its marsh, mud and yachts, so utterly unlike anywhere else in the west of England, existed at all.

He voiced the idea aloud and it met with general approval. It would make a nice change for Rebecca, Cheryl said, but was there a boat? "There was a poster in the Turf," John told her. "I think you go from Topsham."

"The day after tomorrow perhaps? When Macho Man is convalescing."

"What do they actually do to you?" Kevin asked Luke.

"I've no idea, really."

"Maybe they'll give you a vasectomy as well," John said.

"They'd better not! Snip, snip, and my tubes severed."

"Does it make any difference to people's sex lives?" Kevin wondered. "Vasectomy, I mean."

"No. So one is told."

"Extraordinary."

"Why?"

"It scotches the Roman Catholic argument, doesn't it? That sex is only for reproduction. It proves the two functions are not one and the same, pleasure and the ability to have children. I don't mean biologically; I'm not that ignorant! I mean . . . philosophically."

"Yes. You ought to write to the Pope."

"Whoever heard of philosophical sexual pleasures?" John asked.

"Socrates."

"And look what happened to him!"

"Why is that cow staring at me?" Luke wondered. "Moo!" The whole herd looked up for a moment, then returned to the more interesting occupation of eating grass. "What a life! Swishing off flies and standing in sodden fields. Even the grass here is of poor quality. Salty and coarse. But they eat and eat and eat. I eat therefore I am."

"Unlike us," Cheryl said.

"Do I exist because I think? That's like saying you're gay because you think you are. Maybe that's true. Or is it that we're queer because we're queer because we're queer? I'm quoting," he added. "I have learned not to use that word."

"You're drunk," John said.

"A little," he admitted. "Which is a state the cows will never be in."

"A bloody answer for everything! You're becoming a bore."

Perhaps it is time for the barricades, Kevin thought. Not necessarily waving banners or wearing badges, but working out a philosophical position. There is a need to do something more positive than pubs and clubs and discos.

Luke lay on the hospital bed, dressed in a regulation white gown that tied up at the back. Why was there such a rigmarole for what was a very simple operation that took only a few minutes? The curtains were pulled shut round him; a man stood there holding a razor. Luke sat up in alarm. "What's that for?" he said.

The man grinned. "Not what you think. To shave you."

"Shave? Oh, I see. Is it really necessary?"

"Yes. Now if you'll just lie back and lift the gown." Luke did so. "Hmm. Quite a lot, I see. What I call the Old Testament type."

"Old Testament?"

"Prophets and seers. They always looked like forests."

Luke watched him deftly cut away all the hair from the navel down to the top of his legs. It was a humiliating experience; slicing off a great patch of his body hair, making his genitals look like a grotesque parody of a child's, was not something he had imagined beforehand as being part of the procedure. It was an insult! This white square made him feel unmanly. The idea of a lover seeing it! He'd always felt proud of the dark curls that grew from throat to ankle; he remembered, as a teenager, inspecting them to see how thick they were: it was the outward manifestation of his maleness, the sign of superiority over other, less well-endowed men. Childish, of course, to think it meant one was more virile than someone with a bare chest, but Big Luke, prophet and king: now a little rag doll. The downfall of macho male.

"It will grow again," the man said, sensing Luke's consternation.

"I daresay."

What matter now that his penis was bigger than Aaron's, bigger than most he'd seen? It looked absurd, as out of place as moustaches on the Mona Lisa. By the time he was wheeled into the operating theatre he was in a state of deepest gloom.

When he came round from the anaesthetic, surprised to find himself back in the bed, his first thought was to put his hands between his legs : was everything still there? Yes. But he was reminded of the shaved skin. Dozy and drugged, he did not want to move; he shut his eyes, then woke with a start, slept again, woke again, on and off for hours. There was a dull ache in his cock : the conversation about vasectomy returned to his mind. Would he ever have children? He hoped so. It would be strange to be called Dad, instead of using the word oneself. Each stage in life was always a surprise; it never sat on one with total ease : so much of the thinking process was still rooted in the previous department. Roots. Eventually they would grow, like the lost hair. There was still so much to do; his life had hardly begun. Everything so far had been abortive. Cheryl. John. Even at work he hadn't arrived; it was all some kind of preliminary testing-ground for the real thing, whatever that might be. He was still far from being grown-up. When did you reach a place, a time, and say, "Yes, I'm an adult now!" Thirty? Forty? In a month he would be twenty-five, a third of his existence lived. He wanted more and more to be Luke Edwards, our man in Leningrad or La Paz. That was the next crisis, coping with that. He still couldn't bear seeing ITN in case Owen Crawley appeared on the screen; jealousy put him out of humour for days. Though last time he had chuckled. Owen looked desperately seasick in a boat on a very rough sea; an item about taking supplies to a lighthouse that had been cut off for a week by storms and gale force winds. Owen, pale and unhappy, surrounded by weather-beaten sailors used to every moment of it!

The next twenty-five years: as quick as these twenty-five, or quicker people said as you got older, growing more sullen or angry as time passed and the universe remained its same old self? Soon the age his father had died. Dad, who had committed the ultimate of sins: dying because he no longer wanted to live. What shitting on life, on the love his own sons gave him! Was anything worse?

Could it happen again? Nothing was impossible. Dad had actually done it.

But if nothing was impossible, the converse was equally true; there must be a chance to do what Owen was doing, and better. See how others coped with their problems; Jack and Kevin, for instance, had not reached maturity without overcoming a great many more difficulties than he had ever faced. No one had said to him your sexuality is evil and wrong; when he, at twelve or thirteen, became aware of what it was all about and started to fancy girls, it was with no guilt or shame. Not for Jack and Kevin. The straight man didn't have to lead a double life, pretend to his employers or his parents that he was different from what he naturally was, seek out a ghetto of people who had nothing in common but the same sexual orientation, put up with the eternal stream of sneers and innuendos about his kind in almost every newspaper and television programme, remind himself that what masqueraded as liberal and tolerant was not acceptance or understanding. He was lucky to know Jack and Kevin. They educated others by being themselves.

"Cup of tea, Mr Edwards." It was the nurse, a severe no-nonsense type.

"Thank you."

"You can dress and leave as soon as you feel like it."

"But I thought I had to stay in for twenty-four hours. The anaesthetic . . ."

She relaxed. "You've been here twenty-four hours, Mr Edwards!"

"Have I?"

"Never mind. You've slept for a great deal of it. Is someone collecting you?"

Like a parcel, he thought. "No."

"That's all right. As long as you aren't going to drive."

He was going to drive, of course. But he'd manage. At first it was rather unnerving; his reactions were so slow. He stopped on the Brendons, drinking in great drafts of fresh air. If he took it slowly, he'd be fine, at the estuary in just over an hour; resume this interrupted holiday. They'd all be on the beach on a day like this. Rebecca paddling, Cheryl shrieking in the cold water, Jack fooling around. John sunbathing. Kevin building a sandcastle to amuse Rebecca. He felt happy. Then he remembered the ugly white patch, the bare skin he hadn't seen since before he was a teenager. Ridiculous. It would grow, certainly, but it wasn't there *now*.

It was a day when sun and water dissolved everything in light; nothing was solid except the hard wooden seats and the railings of the boat. "There's the cottage," Jack said, quite sure of it, though all he could see was a grey smudge. Light danced in the water, curves, lines, dots that made distance impossible to judge, gave only the river, the boat, the voyage itself any reality.

"Fare forward, travellers," Luke quoted. "The river is within us, the sea is all about us." He was dressed in jeans and a tee-shirt, Jack, Kevin, and Adam in nothing but shorts. It was puzzling; Luke usually enjoyed showing off his body. Kevin, superbly brown, stretched flat on the deck, his legs dangling through the railings, shifting with the motion of the boat. Completely desirable, Jack thought, his eyes constantly reverting to his lover; if he doesn't get up soon I shall screw him in front of all these people. There were twenty or thirty passengers on board, families, holiday-makers.

"The moon!" Rebecca cried. "The moon!"

"Nonsense," Cheryl murmured, not bothering to look up.

But it was, a full moon, so thin and pale it was almost melting into the sky. Lympstone, a collection of houses on the opposite bank to the cottage, usually huddled between two red cliffs like a framed picture, began to separate, to open out into individual buildings, a street, a pub, a grey beach. Ahead was Dawlish Warren, a huge spit of land that centuries of silt had thrown up, and the estuary growing ever wider, the open sea.

Next week he would visit his mother. His father would be at work, unaware. There was no solution. Why such intolerance? It wasn't that uncommon with parents of gays, but Mr Crawley was an extreme case. So it would continue. Deep down the man must hate himself very much to reject his firstling so entirely. He himself would never have children, of course. Not a bitter blow, but . . . well . . . a limitation. It wasn't babies or toddlers he missed; it was when he would be older, without the pleasure of watching the teenage years, the pastimes of early maturity.

Kevin was smoking. The cigarette was stuck in the corner of his mouth, the progress of the boat drifting the smoke along the deck. Sweet, precious boy! Sometimes Jack loved him as one would a wounded bird. But there was no wound.

172

Today I feel quite content just to exist, John said to himself. He was still unable to work : something had burned itself out. Here on this boat, in the hot sun, it didn't matter. A ship of fools. The only reason he was here was because Luke had been staying with him. The day in the hospital at Minehead had been booked before they had split up; if it wasn't for that his ex-lover, too, wouldn't be here. He probably wouldn't see any of these people again; they were Luke's friends, not his. He had been imported into the group, an appendage. Luke, in the future, wouldn't see much of them either; he wasn't destined to spend much time in England during the next few years : John was sure of that. Mogadishu. Luke always got what he wanted. And me? he asked himself. What about me? I suppose I'll be able to work again. Luke hasn't destroyed me. Only I can do that, and I'm not going to.

"Shame we can't see Powderham Castle," Jack said. He looked in the other direction, leaning on the rail, weight on one leg. A strikingly handsome man: women turned their heads when he passed, though he never noticed. Blond hair bleached in the summer sun, brown skin, shorts (white, of course). No woman would ever know the mysteries of his body, what made him the person he was.

"You look happy," Luke said to Kevin.

"I am."

"Like Nogood Boyo."

" 'I don't know who's up there and I don't care'. He was dead right. I'm enjoying a million agreeable sensations. Sun and salt." Luke put his foot in the middle of Kevin's stomach. "Now you've spoiled it. Destroyer!"

Luke laughed, and seeing Adam leave Cheryl's side, he sat on the seat next to her. "First him, now you," she said. "No, that's the wrong way round."

"Don't get us mixed up."

"That's not possible." Her tone was sarcastic.

"What's it like, two brothers?"

"I suppose you mean how do you compare in bed."

"I didn't mean anything of the sort!"

She laughed. "Not that I'd tell you. Not that I even know. He's a different person."

"Tell me something I don't know."

"Why should I?"

"I'm curious."

She squinted up her eyes and looked at him; the sun was directly behind his head. "I don't like you very much," she said.

He smiled. "Don't get hurt again."

"I'm going to have a baby." He stared at her, incredulous.

"But . . . you hardly know each other." She laughed again. "Are you planning to divorce Ron . . . and marry Adam?"

"No."

He ran his hands through his hair, very agitated. "It sounds worse than Oedipus Rex. You could knock me down with . . ."

He stood up and leaned on the rail, looking at distant Starcross with unseeing eyes. Not since he'd discovered his dead father's body that February morning years ago had he felt so amazed and shocked.

The boat was nearing Dawlish Warren. This immense ridge of sand stretching three-quarters of the way across the estuary forced the two-mile width of water into a narrow funnel. It was thick with people, holiday-makers milling about like a swarm of distracted bees. The boat hugged the Starcross side, compelled to do so by the currents and treacherous hidden sandbanks. At last it faced Exmouth, and the town, always neat and compact from the cottage, now spilled out into an ugly urban sprawl. The church was no longer the focal point, lost in a mess of houses, shops, docks, trees, railway lines, winking windows and sky-lights that seemed to have no more pattern or purpose than the clutter of objects on a rubbish tip. Yachts: blue sails, red sails, white sails, tacked and flopped. Hubbub of cars; children, lorries, radios, dogs.

Cheryl enjoyed Luke's bewilderment; it always amused her to see him flounder. Serve him right! Was it inevitable, hankering after him as she had done, that she would turn to another version of him? Adam was a more loving, more caring man. What was still a source of astonishment and delight was that Adam wanted her. He had always known a great deal about her, of course, and he didn't just mean the few times they had gone out together when they were kids. The house in Greenwich, now that Jack and Kevin had gone, they would make their own. No more tenants.

"I need a beer," she said to Rebecca. "I'm thirsty."

As the boat came out from the shelter of the Warren into open water Kevin could observe how river became sea. He sat up. This was what he'd wanted to experience, the join, the mouth. But the sea from here was like a continuation of the estuary, opening wider and wider into a vast emptiness. The familiar things of the shore looked attractive, Hope's Nose, for instance, which was by Torquay, that magical place: magical because of dancing there with Jack, and Jack seeming not to be just a lover but the spring of all good, all energy, a god almost. Maybe they were both a little drunk, yes; but it was there that he'd really fallen in love. It was like dropping over a cliff into a safety-net. In reality, Torquay was not an enchanted place, but quite seedy, with its crime-rate and casinos, its flashy night-clubs. On the other shore were places possibly enchanted because they were unknown and unvisited, the Golden Cap, Lyme, Chesil Beach, Portland Bill. But in between was water — vast, meaningless, frightening. He'd known there would be some significance in this journey, known beforehand it would be more important to him than to the others. Nothing lasts. The estuary becomes the sea; and he knew, quite suddenly but with a blinding certainty, that one day in the future, perhaps not too long in the future, depressed by lack of a job and shut every day in that gilded cage of a cottage on the estuary shore, he would leave Jack, leave him for ever, not once see him again. Jack, the only person he knew whose ability to love did not change, patient and stubborn like the bull of his birth-sign : he would throw this most precious of all gifts away because he was like Aaron and Cheryl and John and Luke, part of the flux, the sea. I've grown up at last, he said to himself. Water. This great empty expanse ahead, so blue and beautiful and glittering in the sunlight, was terrifying. Even the yachts, like paper toys, clung to its edges as if they, too, were appalled.

He needed Jack's arms round him, but fuck it, he was of the same gender; you weren't allowed to do that in public. But Jack, seeing his stricken face, left the rail and came to him. "What is it?" he asked.

He shook his head. "I don't know."

"You're trembling!"

"Yes."

"Sweetheart . . ."

"Hold me. Hold me!"

"I can't. Here."

"I know. Love me. *Always!*"

"I do. And I will."

175

"I love you."

"Kevin. Darling! My life!"

The boat touched land. Busy summer Exmouth. "Now for a beer," Cheryl said.